"It's a hurdle that must be crossed."

Anton went on firmly, "Our marriage will start as I intend it to continue. And you won't find me an insensitive lover."

"No!" Laura cried, shuddering at the intolerable thought of being possessed by him, but at the same time his caressing thumbs on her shoulders were sending a sensuous warmth flowing along her veins.

"I'm your husband, Laura, and before this day has passed I'm going to be your lover. Accept it," he stated harshly and emphatically, "because that's how it will be."

He strode from the room, leaving her alone and more afraid than she'd ever been before. There was no escape from this nightmare she had plunged herself into. She would just have to see it through to the bitter end!

YVONNE WHITTAL
is also the author of these
Harlequin Romances

and this
Harlequin Presents

Many of these titles are available at your local bookseller.

For a free catalogue listing all available Harlequin Romances
and Harlequin Presents, send your name and address to:

HARLEQUIN READER SERVICE,
1440 South Priest Drive, Tempe, AZ 85281
Canadian address: Stratford, Ontario N5A 6W2

Season of Shadows

by

YVONNE WHITTAL

Harlequin Books

TORONTO • LONDON • LOS ANGELES • AMSTERDAM
SYDNEY • HAMBURG • PARIS • STOCKHOLM • ATHENS • TOKYO

Original hardcover edition published in 1980
by Mills & Boon Limited

ISBN 0-373-02430-4

Harlequin edition published September 1981

Printed in U.S.A.

CHAPTER ONE

LAURA HOFFMEYER'S blue eyes were clouded with pain and showed signs of recent tears as she stared out of the aircraft window into the blackness beyond, and tried to come to terms with the shocking reality of what had taken place. She was winging her way from Johannesburg to Cape Town in Anton DeVere's private jet, but the plush white and gold interior of the aircraft went unnoticed as she relived the horrifying events which had taken place since her arrival at her small Hillbrow flat early that evening.

The caretaker had delivered the telegram which had arrived earlier that afternoon, and when the thin, grey-haired woman had departed, Laura stared at the orange-coloured envelope in her hands with a growing uneasiness. Her scatterbrained sister, Elizabeth, sent her a telegram each year on her birthday, but that was still more than two months away, Laura calculated swiftly and, tearing open the envelope, she read the printed message on the official-looking paper within. An icy coldness enveloped her as she read it through several times in order to make sure that her eyes had not deceived her, but the horrifying words remained unchanged.

'*Bluebird wrecked off skeleton coast. No hope of survivors. Sally safe at Bellavista. Come at once. Will telephone travel arrangements at 19h00 sharp. DeVere.*'

As she stood pale and shivering with shock, the telegram had fluttered to the carpeted floor from her nerveless fingers, and then, fighting back the tears while she sought relief in action, she went through to her bedroom and took down a suitcase to start her packing. Later, when she was in control of herself, she telephoned her employer at

7

his home to arrange a week's leave and, when the telephone rang at seven sharp that evening, she was ready to depart at a moment's notice.

'A car will call for you at seven-thirty to drive you out to the Rand Airport where my plane awaits you,' Anton DeVere's deep-throated voice instructed from his home in Cape Town. 'I'll meet you here on your arrival.'

'Sally?' she said quickly, anxious for news of Elizabeth and Robert Dean's ten-year-old daughter before Anton DeVere ended the call in his usual abrupt fashion. 'How did she take it?'

'She was shattered, naturally,' he told her with that familiar hint of impatience in his voice. 'I've put her to bed, but I doubt if she'll sleep until she's seen you.'

There were so many things she had still wanted to know, but she decided reluctantly that they could wait, and their conversation had ended abruptly. In the car driving her at speed to the airport, Laura had shrunk into the shadows on the back seat to give way to the tears she could no longer control, and the driver, if he had heard a suspicious-sounding sniffle coming from behind him, had kept his eyes rigidly on the road ahead.

'Could I bring you something to drink?' a uniformed young man enquired politely, bringing Laura sharply out of her reverie and, at her hesitation, he smiled and added persuasively, 'I can make an excellent cup of tea.'

Laura accepted, realising suddenly that the hollowness at the pit of her stomach was not entirely due to the shock of the news she had received. She had had nothing to eat, or drink, since lunch-time that day, but somehow the thought of food at that moment nauseated her. When the young man returned with her tea she smiled at him grate-fully and, taking that as encouragement, he sat down on the seat opposite her and lit a cigarette which, he told her, was forbidden up front in the cabin and staff quarters.

'Do you know Mr DeVere well?' he asked with eventual curiosity, his openly appreciative glance resting on her honey-brown hair which was coiled into a casual but elegant knot in the nape of her neck.

'I know him well enough to know that he's a man who's so accustomed to having his own way that he could be dangerous when crossed,' she could have said, but instead she said stiffly, 'My sister was married to a very close friend of Mr DeVere's. They were killed this morning when their yacht was wrecked.'

'Oh, I'm sorry,' he said, his sympathetic glance bringing a renewed lump to her throat. 'I'm terribly sorry.'

Laura averted her tear-filled eyes, and the young man, realising that she wanted to be alone, remained only long enough to finish his cigarette before he took her empty cup from her and excused himself.

Anton DeVere's telegram had realised the fears Laura had had since Elizabeth had married Robert Dean. As sisters, with a five-year difference in their ages, they had been close since the death of their parents when Laura had been fourteen. They had been left with sufficient money to support themselves, but, when Elizabeth married Robert a year later, Laura had had no option but to become a boarder at the convent during her last two years at school.

Robert Dean, a wealthy yacht builder from the Cape, had been almost fanatical about his love for the sea and, under his enthusiastic guidance, Elizabeth had developed a wanderlust to match her husband's. The birth of their daughter, Sally, had been almost an inconvenience, but Elizabeth had been determined that nothing would deprive her of her husband's company when he took to the sea in his favourite yacht, *Bluebird*, and Sally had spent her first six years accompanying her parents on their many voyages to foreign continents. She had been able to speak a nautical, seafaring language even before she had been able to speak English, but having to attend boarding school finally curtailed these trips for her, and now, at the age of ten, she had grown into a fiercely independent little creature. Dark-haired, with her father's brown eyes and her mother's smile, Sally occupied a special place in Laura's heart, and it was her concern for the child which succeeded in keeping her dry-eyed and rational now despite her own personal grief.

It was typical of Anton DeVere to take the child into his custody, but Laura had to admit that Bellavista, with its park-like gardens and its splendid view of the wine-producing Constantia valley, was an ideal setting for a child who needed sanctuary while adapting herself to the distressing news that the sea had robbed her of both her beloved parents.

Anton DeVere. Laura shifted her position uncomfortably, almost as if she felt his dominating presence there beside her. She had met him for the first time six years ago while on a visit to her sister, and she had been left with a lasting impression of ruthless strength and raw masculinity. He was the only man who, in all her twenty-six years, somehow had the ability to make her acutely conscious of her femininity merely by being in the same room with her. Cynical and coldly dispassionate, he had treated her initial attempts at friendliness with suspicion and scorn, and through the years, whenever they had met on her frequent visits to Cape Town, she had found herself behaving towards him with a frigid politeness which stemmed from an inexplicable wariness in the company of a man who sometimes had the uncanny knack of reading her mind.

'Please fasten your seat belt, Miss Hoffmeyer,' her thoughts were interrupted apologetically by the young man who had served her tea during the flight. 'We'll be landing in about ten minutes,' he warned.

The two and a half hour flight from Johannesburg to Cape Town was soon at an end, and Laura found herself and her suitcase transported swiftly from the aircraft to the large chauffeur-driven limousine which had driven up moments after the pilot had cut the engines. Anton DeVere stepped from the car at her approach, but she was unaware of the flicker of interest in his hooded eyes as he observed the lithe, easy grace with which she moved. Seeing him again, after an interval of months, was an experience that needed all her self-control, for his tall, wide-shouldered presence exuded that same shattering aura of masculinity which she had encountered at their very first meeting.

'I hope you had a pleasant flight?' he enquired once she was seated beside him in the back of the car and they were being driven from the airport grounds through a private exit.

'The flight was very pleasant, thank you,' she replied stiffly, clasping her hands nervously in her lap as she felt those steel-grey eyes observing her intently in the darkened interior of the car. 'It was very kind of you to place your aircraft at my disposal, Mr DeVere.'

'My concern was for the child,' he brushed aside her remark callously. 'She needs you, so I considered it imperative that I should get you here as quickly as possible.'

That was one way of telling her that she could have gone to the devil as far as he was concerned, Laura thought wryly, but this was one occasion when she would not allow herself to be affected by his cold, autocratic unfriendliness.

'How did it happen?' she asked at last.

'There are plenty of theories, all of them probable, but the most likely one is that, on their way to South America, Robert and Elizabeth were caught up in that freak storm which has been ravaging the west coast during the past few days.' He spoke hurriedly, as if he wanted to get the explanation over and done with as quickly as possible. 'An Air Force helicopter spotted the wreckage early this morning, and there's no doubt that it was the *Bluebird*'s.'

'I don't suppose——'

'No, there's no possibility that they could still be alive somewhere,' he interrupted impatiently, guessing her thoughts, and shattering her final shred of hope. 'The continuation of the search is now a mere formality. There will, of course, be an enquiry afterwards, and only then will their deaths be made official.'

Laura lapsed into silence. She suspected that she had heard as much as he was prepared to tell her at that moment, and any further questions which might occur to her would have to wait until he was in a more amiable mood ... *if* such a thing were possible.

Table Mountain, floodlit and majestic, was ahead of them, and then the car turned off along the freeway towards Constantia, leaving the lights of the city behind them. There was no joy in her surroundings on this occasion, only a deep emptiness and sorrow at the thought that the two people she had loved so dearly would not be there at the end of her journey to welcome her.

'Sally will make up for Elizabeth and Robert's absence,' Anton remarked, sensing her thoughts in that uncanny way of his. His hand found hers briefly in the dark interior of the car, and the touch of those strong fingers gripping her own was as unexpected as it was comforting.

The car swept through the gates of Bellavista and up the long avenue of cypress trees towards the two-storied, gabled house which was surrounded by spacious, beautifully kept gardens which were now shrouded in darkness.

This was not Laura's first visit to Anton DeVere's impressive home. She had been there once before with Robert and Elizabeth when Anton had entertained a client on a visit from Germany. It had been an all-day affair with swimming in the marble pool, and tennis on Bellavista's two excellent courts. A typical South African *braai* had been arranged for that evening, and afterwards the long dining hall had been cleared for dancing. Laura had not lacked partners that evening, but Anton had never once asked her to dance, and his obvious omission had strengthened her suspicion that she had been there on sufferance because of the family tie between herself and the wife of his closest friend.

The car drew up beside the shallow steps leading up to the double oak doors, and moments later Laura found herself in Bellavista's large entrance hall with its original black and white stone floor still in perfect, gleaming condition. Small Persian rugs lay scattered decoratively on the floor, while a carved wooden bench and an antique rosewood table were the only other objects to adorn the hall, she noticed when she cast a swift, appreciative glance about her.

'Sally's room is this way,' Anton announced, and she was led across the hall, up the curved staircase, down a passage and along yet another before he opened a door and stood aside for her to enter. 'This is your room,' he said, not giving her the opportunity to look about her before he opened the interleading door and ushered her into the adjoining room.

A bedside lamp illuminated the room and a child sat up eagerly in the bed the moment they entered through the door.

'Aunty Laura?' she whimpered pathetically, her eyes red and swollen, and Laura went to her at once, seating herself on the side of the bed as she leaned forward to take the child into her arms and hold her close.

'Sally darling!' Laura exclaimed softly, controlling her own desire to weep as she felt the small, firm body in her arms shaking with the force of her tears.

'They're d-dead, Aunty Laura,' Sally sobbed brokenly into Laura's neck. 'M-Mummy and D-Daddy are d-dead.'

'I know, darling, I know,' Laura whispered, brushing a strand of dark hair out of Sally's eyes and kissing the wet, flushed cheek to hide the moisture in her own eyes.

'Why, Aunty Laura?' Sally cried. 'Why did they have to die?'

Laura swallowed convulsively to relieve the ache in her throat and tightened her arms about her young niece. 'I can't answer that, Sally, but for all of us there's a time to live and a time to die, and we must accept that God wanted it this way.'

'I wish I were dead too!'

'Don't wish that, darling,' Laura cautioned swiftly with

a lump in her throat. 'You're all I have now.'

'You should go to sleep now, Sally,' Anton instructed, speaking for the first time since they had entered the room, and Laura felt almost guilty at having forgotten his existence for those few brief moments. 'It's been a long day for you,' he added sternly, 'and you must get some rest.'

'Yes, Uncle Anton,' Sally whispered, sliding beneath the covers, but her anxious glance returned swiftly to Laura. 'You'll be here tomorrow when I wake up?'

'I'll be here,' Laura promised, and the plea in Sally's eyes wrenched at her heart as she leaned forward to kiss her on the forehead.

Later, in the living-room with its stone fireplace and priceless seventeenth-century furniture, Anton poured coffee and extended a silver salver towards her.

'Have a sandwich,' he ordered.

'I'm not——'

'I doubt if you had anything to eat this evening,' he observed dryly, his cold grey eyes narrowing at the look of guilt that flashed across her pale, sensitive face. 'I thought not,' he added reprovingly before she could think up a reply.

'I wasn't very hungry,' Laura explained lamely, accepting a sandwich much against her will.

'Neither was I,' he stated calmly, placing the salver on the low table between them and helping himself. 'I was also too busy to take time off for dinner this evening.'

Laura bit into the tastily prepared chicken sandwich, and was surprised to discover how hungry she actually was. The sandwiches disappeared rapidly, and while they ate, she observed the man reclining in the armchair opposite her. The silver threads in his dark hair had become more pronounced since their last meeting, but the tanned, angular face with the hawklike nose still wore that mask of ruthlessness she remembered so well. There was nothing attractive about the hard set of his mouth and jaw, but there was that indefinable quality about him that reminded her of a sleek panther, always on the alert, and with those powerful muscles geared for action at a moment's notice to claim its terrified prey. Perhaps it was that quality of danger about him which had first stirred her senses and made her so aware of him that she had never quite succeeded in forgetting him, she thought ruefully.

Anton DeVere was a man apart; an enigma, and, as the head of DeVere Enterprises, she was certain that he would never quite realise the total extent of his wealth. He was far beyond her reach, and even if she had ever been foolish enough to hope for something more in their relationship—which she had not—then she had known from their first meeting the futility of it. With Elizabeth and Robert no longer there, she would, in all probability, never meet him again after this, and the realisation left her with the curious sensation that she was in the process of losing something of value.

'More coffee?' Anton interrupted her thoughts, and she lowered her lashes swiftly to conceal what was mirrored in the depths of her deep blue eyes, but she could not conceal the guilty flush that stole up into her cheeks at the thought of how close she had come to being caught staring.

'No, thank you,' she said with frigid politeness. 'No more coffee for me.'

'Cigarette?'

'Please,' she nodded, leaning forward to accept a cigarette from him.

Laura seldom smoked, except in moments of stress, and this, she felt, was one of those moments. She had grown tense with concern for her niece, and the knowledge that she had to be strong for the child's sake. The shock of Elizabeth and Robert's deaths had had to take second place, but she felt it now in every taut muscle as she sat in Bellavista's luxuriously furnished living-room, smoking her cigarette in thoughtful silence. She felt Anton's eyes on her, invading the turmoil of her unhappy thoughts, and she said the first thing that came into her mind when the silence between them became unnerving.

'Do you think their bodies will ever be recovered?'

'I doubt it,' Anton replied without hesitation. 'The sea nearly always holds on to its own.'

'It's a distressing thought,' she said unsteadily, crushing her half-smoked cigarette into the ashtray beside her chair.

'It's a very appropriate burial ground for two people who loved the sea as much as they did.'

'I think I'd like to go to bed,' she said at once, unable to bear the idea of two such vital people lying fathoms deep somewhere under the ocean, and Anton rose politely to wish her goodnight, but at the door she paused and turned. 'I hope you don't mind, but I'd like to stay until the end of next week. There's Sally's future to think about, and——'

'You may stay as long as you wish,' Anton interrupted in that firm, autocratic voice, 'but Sally's future has already been decided.'

Laura felt a new tightness coiling about her insides. 'What do you mean, her future has already been decided?'

He dismissed her query with an imperious wave of his hand, but when she stood her ground, he said harshly, 'I think we'll leave that discussion for the morning when we're both less tired.'

'But I insist on knowing!'

Except for a slight narrowing of those heavy-lidded steel-grey eyes, his granite-like expression remained unaltered, but Laura knew at once that she had overstepped the mark.

'You are not in a position to insist upon anything,' he reminded her coldly. 'It's I who am insisting that you retire to your room and leave me to the privacy I'm accustomed to.'

Laura felt very much like a child who had been rapped severely over the knuckles, and, as the blood surged painfully into her cheeks, she realised that, despite his hospitality and the generosity of his efforts to bring her to Sally's side, Anton DeVere still considered her an intruder. She wished she knew why this knowledge should hurt so much, but she was not going to hang around to find out and, muttering a hasty 'goodnight', she managed to find her way back to the room she was to occupy for the next few days.

There was no sign of her suitcase, but, to her astonishment, she discovered that her clothes had been transferred neatly to the stinkwood wardrobe and dresser in the room. The satin quilt had been removed from the old-fashioned copper bed, and her thin cotton nightgown had been folded and placed neatly on the pillows.

She entered Sally's room quietly and found that she was sleeping soundly with her one hand curled beneath her cheek. Laura stood looking down at her with sympathetic concern until a warm tenderness threatened to choke her and, drawing a steadying breath, she turned away and returned quietly to her own room.

In the adjoining bathroom she soaked herself in a hot bath until she felt the aching tension drain from her body, but reaction set in when she eventually put out the light and climbed into bed. Choking sobs racked her body, and she buried her face in the pillows to stifle the sound of her tears for fear of disturbing Sally. Laura had felt it coming since her arrival in Cape Town, but somehow she had managed to keep it in check until now. She had been terrified, also, of making a fool of herself in her imperious host's presence, but she had thankfully been spared that humiliating experience.

When the storm of her weeping finally ceased, Laura slipped into an exhausted sleep from which she did not awake until a light hand touched her shoulder the following morning. She opened her eyes reluctantly to find herself staring into two accusing brown eyes.

'I've been waiting ages for you to wake up,' Sally announced with a hint of impatience in her voice.

Laura sat up at once and stifled a yawn. 'What time is it?'

'It's half past eight,' Sally informed her, perching on the side of the bed and flicking her long plaits over her shoulders. 'I had breakfast with Uncle Anton before he went to the office, and he said I was not to wake you until now because you were very tired last night.' Laura could not quite make up her mind whether to feel touched or displeased by that remark, but she allowed it to pass when she noticed a suspicion of tears in Sally's eyes. 'I'm so glad you came, Aunty Laura.'

Laura opened her arms wide, and Sally almost fell into them. 'Did you think I would stay away when I knew that you needed me, darling?' she asked with her cheek pressed against the smooth dark head resting on her shoulder.

'No, but ...' Sally paused and tightened her arms about Laura. 'You're always such fun to be with, and—and when I'm with you I know I—I shan't feel as though Mummy is so far from me.'

Her childish logic was touching, and Laura stared beyond Sally at the patch of sunlight on the floor, vowing to herself that she would bring the sparkle back into her niece's eyes, and the laughter to that drooping little mouth.

'I'll go and tell Jemima you're awake so that she can make your breakfast, then I'll come back to show you the way to the breakfast-room,' Sally announced eagerly as she extricated herself from Laura's arms and made for the door.

'Sally, wait!' Laura called after her. 'I don't want much to eat. Just a slice of toast and a cup of coffee will do.'

'Okay,' Sally nodded, slamming the door behind her in her haste.

Laura washed and dressed quickly before she brushed and coiled her hair into its usual knot. Shadows still lurked in her usually clear blue eyes, and there was an unusual tightness about the soft, generous mouth when she applied a touch of lipstick to it. Her mind had conjured up a remembered vision of a man and a woman, their happy laughter drifting towards her on the breeze as she watched them standing with their arms wrapped about each other. Robert and Elizabeth had been crazy about each other, almost to the exclusion of their daughter, Sally, but the child had somehow never been made to feel in the way. Their love for each other had been something unique; a once-in-a-lifetime thing. The one would have been totally lost without the other, and it was almost a blessing that fate had decreed they should die together.

She shivered and shed her morbid thoughts with a hasty effort when Sally burst into the room, and then she was following the child through the house with its priceless collection of antiques.

The breakfast-room was spacious and sunny, and Laura had barely seated herself at the large table when a woman pushed a laden trolley into the room. Her spotless white apron almost crackled as she moved, and her dark eyes summed Laura up in a friendly, interested fashion, then white teeth flashed in a smile.

'Good morning, Miss Laura,' she said politely.

'Good morning ... er ... Jemima?'

'That's right, miss.'

'Did *you* unpack my suitcase for me last night?' Laura enquired curiously.

'Yes, Miss Laura.'

'That was very kind of you,' Laura thanked her, but when she observed the contents of the dishes being transferred from the trolley on to the table, her eyes widened in dismay. There seemed to be enough there to feed half a dozen hungry men, she thought with a touch of humour as she eyed the amount of eggs, bacon, fried tomatoes and steak. 'Good heavens, Jemima,' she exclaimed at last, 'I'll never be able to eat all that!'

'It's Mr Anton's orders, Miss Laura,' Jemima announced emphatically. 'He said, "See that Miss Laura has a good breakfast. She can't live on sandwiches alone." That's what he said.'

'You'll have to eat it, Aunty Laura,' Sally warned, seating herself on the chair beside Laura and resting her elbows on the table. 'Uncle Anton gets awfully furious if his orders aren't carried out.'

Uncle Anton could go hopping for all she cared, Laura thought irritably, but it was the thought of Jemima being caught in the backwash of his anger that brought her swiftly to her senses.

'It seems I have no choice, then, so I'll just have to do the best I can,' she replied, eyeing the food dubiously. 'Thank you, Jemima, for all your trouble.'

'No trouble, Miss Laura,' the woman assured her with that flashing smile that lit up her dark eyes. 'But there *will* be trouble if Mr. Anton finds out that I had to take it all back to the kitchen.'

Some minutes later Laura discovered, to her amazement, that she was actually hungry, and with a certain amount of assistance from Sally, the serving dishes were practically empty when they were eventually wheeled back to the kitchen by a beaming Jemima.

Bellavista lay high up in the curve of the mountain, and when Laura went for a walk with Sally through the grounds among the cedar, beech, and olive trees, she could almost forget what had brought her so unexpectedly from the concrete jungle of Johannesburg to the peace and tranquillity of the Constantia valley. Sparrows and buntings fluttered noisily in the trees, while a turtle dove called from somewhere to its mate in the branches overhead. Butterflies flitted back and forth among the bright yellow chrysanthemums while the sun climbed higher in the clear blue sky and, as they approached the ornamental well, they disturbed the lazy, early-morning siesta of a small, sleek lizard, and it scurried off the stone wall to disappear into the undergrowth.

Laura channelled the conversation with her young niece into avenues free from grief, but they inevitably led back to the events of the day before.

'Uncle Anton fetched me out of boarding school early yesterday morning, and the headmistress gave permission for me not to attend school these two days before the weekend.' Sally kicked listlessly at a pebble while she spoke. 'I have to go back to school on Monday, but for the rest of the term, until the March holidays, I'll be a day scholar.'

'And after the holidays?' Laura prompted curiously.

Sally shrugged in a surprisingly adult fashion. 'Uncle Anton said that, when the holidays were over, he would decide what to do about me.'

So Sally's future was not as decided as Anton DeVere had wanted her to believe, Laura reflected wryly. She would have to speak to him again about the child, and soon it seemed, in order to make the necessary arrangements for their flight back to Johannesburg. She wanted Sally with her; as her aunt she had that right, and Anton DeVere was not in a position to prevent it.

A small hand gripped her fingers tightly. 'Don't leave me, Aunty Laura.'

Laura smiled confidently down into those anxious brown eyes, and made a promise she was to regret bitterly in the not too distant future. 'I shan't ever leave you, Sally, and that's a promise.'

A look of relief flashed across the child's face, and she smiled for the first time as she released Laura's hand and ran towards the kidney-shaped pool with her plaits bobbing down her back. The water looked cool and inviting on that humid summer morning and, when Sally suggested a swim, Laura blessed the fact that she had remembered to pack her swimsuit almost at the last moment.

They went indoors to change, but when they emerged some minutes later Laura saw a slight young man approaching the house. Tightening the belt of her towelling robe about her waist, she sent Sally on ahead to the pool while she herself remained on the terrace to await the arrival of their unexpected visitor.

'Good morning,' the man smiled as he leapt eagerly up the steps towards Laura, his keen, alert eyes taking in her slenderness, and the length of her tanned, shapely legs beneath the hem of her short robe. 'Miss Laura Hoffmeyer?' he asked at last, meeting her steady blue gaze with a hint of familiarity in his glance that made her stiffen with distaste.

'That's right,' she said abruptly, wondering how he knew her name, and when he made no effort to introduce himself, she asked, 'Have we met before?'

'I don't think so,' he smiled ruefully, casting another swift glance down the length of her before he explained 'I'm from the press, Miss Hoffmeyer, and——'

'Are you here with Mr DeVere's knowledge?' she interrupted hastily, not quite certain how to handle a situation such as this.

'Not with Mr DeVere's knowledge, no,' the man admitted unashamedly, 'but I don't imagine he will object to my asking you a few questions in connection with the accident which involved your sister and brother-in-law.'

'I suggest you approach Mr DeVere for the information you require, but, as he isn't here at the moment, I think it would be advisable if you left the way you came.'

Ignoring her remark, he flicked open his notebook and held his pen in readiness. 'Miss Hoffmeyer, is there any truth in the rumour that Robert Dean was on a secret mission for the government?'

'Secret mission?' Startled, Laura stared at him, not quite certain whether to laugh, or be angry. 'What are you talking about?'

'Come now, Miss Hoffmeyer, you must have known something about it?'

'I assure you, I——'

'There are also rumours that it was an explosion on board the *Bluebird* which caused the deaths of Robert Dean and his wife,' the infuriating man continued blandly, and Laura felt as though she had been dealt a shattering blow to her midriff. 'Is there any truth in this rumour?' he persisted uncaringly.

'None whatsoever,' a deep-throated, autocratic voice replied coldly, and Laura turned blindly towards the man who had joined them on the terrace.

'Anton!'

CHAPTER TWO

THE world tilted and swivelled at a sickening pace about
Laura as she swayed towards Anton, and a hard, steadying
arm was instantly placed about her slim shoulders during
the frightening silence which followed his arrival.

The cocky young reporter seemed unperturbed, however,
by the imperious presence of the master of Bellavista. 'Mr
DeVere, I'm from the press, and I wonder if you
would——'

'You can stop wondering and get off my property,'
Anton ordered harshly.

'I'm only doing my duty, Mr DeVere. Robert Dean's
death is news, and I——'

'Find your news elsewhere,' Anton interrupted in an icy
voice that made Laura feel thankful that she was not at the
receiving end of it. 'You're here without my authorised
permission, and I call that a blatant invasion of my
privacy. Now, get off my property, and make it snappy
before I order my man to see you off the premises.' The
young man stood his ground with a fearlessness Laura
could not help admiring until Anton glanced back over his
shoulder and rapped out, 'Eddie!'

A bulky, well-muscled man appeared in the doorway behind them, and, as he advanced, the young reporter retreated hastily.

'All right, I'm going,' he said resignedly, hurrying down
the steps and heading towards the driveway, but Anton was
taking no chances and he gestured Eddie to follow him to
make certain of his departure.

'Anton, what was all that about?' she asked after a
moment, moving selfconsciously from the solid circle of his
arm.

'Nothing you need concern yourself with.'

'But he insinuated that Robert had been on a secret mission, and that there'd been an explosion on board——'

'Forget it,' he cut in harshly, but Laura felt driven to get to the bottom of the reporter's odd remarks.

'Was he merely seeking sensationalism where there was none, or was there some truth in his insinuating questions?'

'I said forget it!'

'I *can't* forget it!' she cried chokingly, her hands clenched at her sides as she tried to control the shudders that rippled through her body, and her glance was imploring as she added shakily, 'Anton, I have a right to know the truth.'

The air was tense between them and, for a moment, she thought he was going to refuse, then he gestured grimly towards the wooden bench against the whitewashed wall. 'Let's sit down over there.'

He offered her a cigarette and, when she refused, he lit one for himself and drew on it deeply. She sat there stiffly beside him, her hands clasped tightly in her lap as she waited to hear what he had to say, but she knew, with a deadly certainty, that he would merely be giving her a more detailed version of what she already knew.

'Robert *was* on a secret mission,' Anton admitted finally in clipped, decisive tones. 'Not to South America as I led you to believe, but to a country I'm not at liberty to mention. The information leaked out somehow, and made its way into the wrong hands. An anonymous caller telephoned Defence Headquarters early yesterday morning, tipping them off about the bomb which had been placed on board the *Bluebird*, and a bomb disposal team was flown out in a helicopter.' He drew hard on his cigarette and blew the smoke forcibly into the air, but his action relayed a suppressed violence she felt certain he would not hesitate to unleash if he could get his hands on the culprits. 'They arrived seconds too late,' he added harshly.

'Why was this information not transmitted through to

Robert on the radio?' she wanted to know, helpless anger rising within her at what she suspected was gross negligence on the part of the proper authorities. 'It would have given them time to abandon the yacht, and——'

'They couldn't contact them,' Anton interrupted. 'The bomb was connected to the radio, and whoever planted it there knew that Robert would maintain radio silence until seven yesterday morning when he was well out to sea from Walvis Bay. The moment the radio was activated with incoming or outgoing calls, the bomb would be detonated, and that left us with no choice but to try to reach them in time.' He rose suddenly and flicked his cigarette angrily over the low wall. 'The whole operation was futile from the start, and I warned Robert against it, but he insisted on going.'

'Why did Elizabeth accompany him on this mission?' she asked, her unreasonable anger subsiding and leaving her feeling a little ashamed of herself.

'You know as well as I do that Robert never went anywhere without his wife,' he explained, thrusting his hands into the pockets of his impeccably tailored dark suit as he stood with his back turned towards her. 'There seemed to be no reason why she should stay behind on this occasion, and no one, not even I, suspected that there would be any real danger involved in what he was about to do.'

'Did Elizabeth know the purpose of his mission?'

'I'm certain she did.'

Laura realised now, with sickening clarity, why he had been so adamant about their bodies never being recovered, and as she stared up at his broad back she wished that she could leave the matter there, but there was one more question she had to ask. 'Why did you want to hide the truth from me? I can understand why it's best to keep it from Sally, but why from me?'

'I hoped you would never have to know,' he said, turning to face her, and as she searched his chiselled features in an effort to understand his reasoning, he added abruptly,

'What you don't know, you can't divulge to others.'

Her anger rose sharply at the obvious insult. 'Just what do you think I am?'

'Don't jump to conclusions,' he ordered sharply. 'I've just told you that there was more danger involved in that mission than anyone realised, that's why there's safety in total ignorance.'

'Safety?' she echoed stupidly, then her eyes widened as comprehension dawned and brought with it a certain amount of fear. 'You mean I—I can't be forced to speak of something I know nothing about?'

His mouth hardened. 'Exactly.'

'The situation is still dangerous, then?' she asked unsteadily, a cold shiver racing up her spine.

'It could be, but we're taking no chances.'

'We?' she queried, but Anton's shuttered expression warned her that she was beginning to pry too deeply. 'I'm sorry,' she muttered apologetically. 'And thank you for telling me as much as you have.'

She held her breath, trying to decide whether to feel afraid or not, and then the awkward silence was shattered by the sound of running footsteps on the path below the terrace.

'I thought you were coming for a swim,' Sally demanded of Laura with a well-remembered haughtiness as she skipped up the steps.

'Yes ... well, I ...' Laura flashed an appealing glance in Anton's direction, and he reacted in a most surprising way.

'If you give me a couple of minutes, then I'll join the two of you for that swim,' he announced, removing his tie as he entered the house through the double glass doors.

'Don't be long, Uncle Anton,' Sally called after him and, taking Laura's hand, she said: 'Come on, the water is lovely.'

Sally swam well, Laura noticed as she floated lazily on her back in the cool, refreshing water. Robert Dean and her sister had made certain that their daughter could swim

before she was a year old, which was just as well, Laura
thought wryly, considering that the yacht had practically
been the child's home.

She closed her eyes for a moment to shut out painful
memories, but when she opened them again she found herself staring up at Anton who stood poised on the edge of
the pool. Long-limbed, tanned and muscular in his blue
swimming briefs, she was again made aware of that quality
of steel in him; that ruthless strength which had somehow
always frightened her. To have him as her enemy was
something she prayed would never happen, for Anton
DeVere would be merciless in his attack.

Steel-grey eyes mocked her as if he knew every single
thought that raced through her mind, and then he was
diving into the water, his body moving beneath the surface
with eel-like swiftness in her direction. Her heart hammered and her throat tightened with something close to
panic as she tried to get away, but she felt like a helpless in-
fant thrashing at the water. Strong hands encircled her
waist, and a little cry of terror passed her lips before she
could prevent it from doing so.

Anton was not indulging in a foolish prank, she realised
at once when he emerged behind her. The roughness of his
hard chest was against her back, and the hands about her
waist tightened almost threateningly as he hissed into her
ear, 'Remember ... not a word to Sally of the information
I passed on to you. Not a word to anyone, in fact.'

'Of course not!' she whispered back indignantly, angered
that he should have thought it necessary to remind her,
and then she was released.

'Race you to the other side, Uncle Anton,' Sally challenged, and then Laura was left to continue with her
leisurely swim, but somehow the pleasure had gone out of
it.

Jemima eventually served them with iced lemonade, and
they sipped at it appreciatively while they dried themselves
in the sun.

'Are you going back to the office after lunch, Uncle Anton?' Sally wanted to know.

'No,' he smiled faintly, tugging playfully at one wet pigtail. 'I thought we might take a drive out to Bloubergstrand.'

There was a terrifying little silence during which only the chattering of the birds in the trees could be heard, then Sally asked hesitantly, 'Are we going to the cottage?'

'Yes.' Anton drained his glass and placed it in the tray. 'Would you like to go?' he asked casually, giving the impression that he did not care whether she went or not, but when Sally finally nodded, that faint smile was again noticeable about his hard mouth.

The drive out to Blougergstrand did not take long that afternoon, and on this occasion they did not travel in the long black chauffeur-driven limousine which had met Laura at the airport, but in a white Jaguar with Anton driving himself. His hands were relaxed on the wheel, and fine dark hairs curled about the gold wrist watch which had emerged from the sleeve of his grey lightweight jacket. He had nice hands, she decided absently. They were broad and strong, with clipped, clean fingernails.

Sally sat quietly in the back of the car, but when Anton parked the car at the gate of the whitewashed cottage, there was a frown between her dark brows and a tightness about her small mouth that disturbed Laura.

From almost every window in the cottage one could look out across the ten-kilometre stretch of Table Bay at the most photographed view of Table Mountain with the city sprawled out below it. It was a view she would never tire of, she thought as she recalled looking out of the bedroom window one spring morning to see a carpet of colourful wild flowers covering the sand dunes.

'Why don't you get the rest of your things together so we can take them back to Bellavista when we leave?' Anton suggested to Sally as he unlocked the front door and stood aside for them to enter.

'Okay,' Sally replied listlessly and, not wanting to leave her alone in this mood, Laura followed her to her room.

She helped the child pack some of her belongings into suitcases and an empty box which they found in the kitchen, but when Sally eventually said stiffly, 'I can manage on my own,' Laura realised that she was intruding on Sally's last moments in the home she would never enter again, and she left her reluctantly to go in search of Anton.

She found him in Robert's study, searching through the desk drawers, and he looked up with a noticeable start when she entered the room and asked curiously, 'What are you looking for?'

'Anything and everything which I may have missed yesterday, and which might connect Robert with the mission he was on.'

Laura shivered involuntarily. 'I'm beginning to feel as if I've leapt into the middle of a James Bond movie.' Her foot kicked against an object lying half hidden beside the desk, and she bent down quickly to retrieve it. 'Here's something. It looks like a map of sorts.'

'That's it!' he said sharply, almost snatching the folded paper from her hands to examine it. Satisfied that he had found what he had been looking for, he dropped the map into the grate and set it alight. The paper discoloured and curled as it turned into ashes, and as the last flame flickered and died, he turned and asked abruptly, 'Why aren't you helping Sally?'

Laura's back stiffened with annoyance. 'She wanted to be alone, but if you feel I'm in the way——'

'Don't be so touchy, dammit!' he growled irritably, taking a flat gold case from his jacket pocket and flicking it open. 'Cigarette?'

'No, thank you.'

She turned away towards the window while he lit a cigarette for himself and stood smoking it in silence beside the fireplace. Laura felt choked and close to tears as she stared out across the bay. Being in the cottage among the bric-à-brac Elizabeth and Robert had collected together over the years was an unbearably painful experience, and it forced upon her the stark finality of death.

'There's something about you which has always puzzled me,' Anton's voice invaded her thoughts, and she controlled herself forcibly before she turned to face him questioningly. 'Why is an attractive girl like yourself not married yet?' he asked unexpectedly.

Laura stiffened and replied daringly, 'I could ask you a similar question.'

'I've never found a woman whom I thought I could spend the rest of my life with.' His eyes were narrowed and mocking beneath the heavy eyebrows. 'Now it's your turn.'

'I haven't met the right man yet.'

'You've known several men?'

She looked away from his curiously penetrating gaze and coloured slightly. 'A few.'

'Were they passionate affairs?'

'Certainly not!' she exclaimed indignantly, her colour heightened by the gleam of sardonic amusement in his eyes. 'I don't believe in—in that sort of thing.'

'Why not?' he laughed shortly, flinging the remainder of his cigarette into the grate. 'Are you afraid of sex?'

Laura drew an audible breath, and lowered her eyes as she said furiously, 'I refuse to continue this outrageous conversation.'

'There's nothing outrageous about sex,' he persisted blandly.

'I never said there was,' she replied defensively, 'but I have no desire to indulge in a sexual affair with any man unless I'm married to him.'

His mouth twisted cynically. 'Chastity in unmarried women went out of fashion years ago.'

'I wouldn't be so ready to believe that, if I were you,' she retorted hotly, her blue eyes sparkling with anger. 'It's more likely that you've met all the wrong kind of women.'

'I've always found women very easily persuaded to relinquish their virginity.' His glance was an intolerable insult as it roamed over her with a deliberate slowness that left her with the shattering sensation that he was stripping her mentally, and then, to add to her embarrassment, his mouth curved into a sensuous smile as if he had enjoyed what he had seen. 'If a man with the right amount of experience came along, you might find yourself equally eager to lose what you now pride yourself in possessing.'

Her slim body went taut with resentment. 'When you speak of a man with the right amount of experience, I presume you're referring to yourself?'

'Possibly.' The lazy, sensuous smile still hovered infuriatingly about his mouth, but those razor-sharp eyes were quick to notice that treacherous little pulse throbbing madly at the base of her throat. 'Does the thought excite you?'

'I think you're despicable!' she exclaimed angrily, for once not afraid of him as she felt herself blushing to the roots of her hair.

'Perhaps I am,' he admitted, his expression becoming decidedly bored as he seated himself on the corner of the desk and crossed his arms over his chest. 'It was one way, though, of making you forget your surroundings for a time, and the tragic circumstances which have brought you here.'

'Do you mean to say you were baiting me deliberately?' she demanded with a mixture of incredulity and anger.

'You could say so, yes,' he admitted without the slightest sign of regret.

Laura was speechless for a moment as she stood with her hands clenched tightly at her sides in an effort to suppress the mad desire to strike him, then the words seemed to tumble from her lips. 'I think you're the most detestable man I've ever had the misfortune to meet!'

During the electrifying silence which followed her outburst, his eyes pierced her like steel blades, and she realised, too late, what she had said, and to whom, but, while she still struggled to formulate an apology, an in-credulous voice demanded from just inside the study door, 'Are you two fighting?'

For a moment neither of them moved, then his expression cleared miraculously as he turned to look at the little girl who stood hovering nervously in the doorway. 'You could say we were having a slight difference of opinion, Sally,' he explained with surprising affability. 'Are you ready to leave?'

Sally stared at them with a measure of uncertainty, then she nodded her dark head, and said: 'Yes, I've got everything.'

'Good,' he nodded abruptly, and a few minutes later they were driving back to Bellavista, leaving behind a locked and shuttered cottage filled with personal reminders of the two people who had once lived, and loved, there.

After dinner that evening, when Sally had gone to bed, Laura joined Anton in the living-room in a grimly deter-mined effort to discuss her plans for the child. His long, virile body was sprawled lazily in a chair, and his eyes were closed when she entered, but she had barely walked a few paces into the room when she found his cool, cal-culating glance fixed intently upon herself, and for one frightening moment her courage almost deserted her.

'I'd like to talk to you about Sally,' she said in a rush before she had time to change her mind.

'Ah, yes, Sally's future,' he remarked slowly, looking thoroughly bored as he gestured vaguely that she should sit down.

Laura seated herself stiffly on the edge of the chair fac-ing him, and tried not to look as nervous as she was feel-ing at that moment when she said: 'I want to take Sally back to Johannesburg with me.'

'I'm afraid that's out of the question,' he replied evenly. 'Sally will remain here at Bellavista with me where I can keep an eye on her.'

'I don't think you have any right to dictate her future,' she argued tritely, hating his superbly confident manner. 'I'm her aunt; her only living relative, and——'

'And I'm her guardian,' he cut in smoothly.

She sucked her breath in sharply, her eyes widening in incredulous disbelief. 'You're her *what*?'

'You heard me.'

'But that's absurd!'

'Is it?' he smiled, but the smile never touched those cold, heavy-lidded eyes, and she shuddered at the thought of Sally being placed in the care of a man who was so totally without the necessary compassion and sensitivity.

'A man can't possibly see to all the needs of a girl Sally's age,' she argued desperately, gripping her hands tightly in her lap to hide the fact that they were shaking.

'She will enjoy the safety of my home, the best schools in the country, and my entire staff here at Bellavista will be at her disposal to pander to her needs when she's not at school.' Those steel-grey eyes beneath the heavy brows seemed to be viewing her with a calculating coldness filled with contempt. 'What can you offer Sally? A small flat in Hillbrow where she'll spend most of her time alone and without supervision while you're at work?'

'But I——'

'You have my permission to come and see her whenever you wish, but, as her legally appointed guardian, I insist that she remains here.'

There was a sinking feeling at the pit of Laura's stomach when she heard that deadly finality in his voice, and what she hated most was the knowledge that he had been right. Sally would have more freedom here at Bellavista in comparison with children living in the cosmopolitan flat-land of Johannesburg, and, financially, she was ill equipped to offer Sally the kind of life she was accustomed to; the kind of life Anton DeVere could offer her even without the considerable amount Sally would eventually inherit from her father's estate.

Laura's mind darted this way and that, frantically seeking a loophole in order to fulfil the promise she had made Sally, but she knew in her heart that, legally, she did not stand a chance against someone as wealthy and influential as Anton DeVere, and she reluctantly had to admit defeat.

'Much as I would have wanted her with me, it seems as though I have no choice but to leave her in your care,' she sighed at length, biting down hard on her quivering lip, and avoiding those probing eyes. 'If you're certain that my staying here won't inconvenience you, then I'll make arrangements to return to Johannesburg next Friday as planned.'

'My private aircraft will be at your disposal whenever you wish to return.'

'No *no*, Aunty Laura! You *can't* leave me! You *promised*!' Laura leapt to her feet at the sound of Sally's voice, almost losing her balance as the child hurtled across the room directly into her arms to cling to her desperately while she cried wildly and hysterically, 'Tell, her, Uncle Anton! Tell her she has to stay. You *can't* leave me. I won't let you. I *won't* let you go!'

Laura was vaguely aware that Anton had risen quickly from his chair, but she was too alarmed by the sobbing, hysterical child in her arms to hear what he was saying.

'Sally, don't!' she ordered sharply, stroking the dark head soothingly. 'Stop it, do you hear me? Stop it! You'll make yourself ill!'

A heavy hand came down on to Laura's shoulder and gripped hard. 'Get her upstairs. I'll call the doctor.'

Slight of build and strength, Laura managed somehow to get Sally up to her room, but the hysterical weeping did not cease even when she sat on the bed with the child in her arms.

'Don't leave me, Aunty Laura,' Sally pleaded repeatedly, her eyes wild in her damp, flushed face. 'Don't leave me. You *promised*!'

'Calm down, darling. Calm down,' Laura tried to pacify her, but nothing she could do, or say, seemed to have the desired effect on Sally. She could not repeat the foolish promise she had made, knowing now that she could not fulfil it, and she was almost frantic with concern and despair when Anton entered the room some minutes later with a tall, thin, grey-haired man.

'Dr Abbot!' Sally almost screamed his name, releasing her frantic grip on Laura for the first time and quite literally throwing herself at the man who approached the bed.

'There now, young Sally,' he said lightly, lowering her on to the bed, and placing the back of his fingers against the child's burning cheeks. 'I think you and I should have a quiet little chat ... hm?'

'We'll wait downstairs,' Anton announced and, taking Laura's arm, he marched her firmly from the room.

She tried to shake off his hand, but his fingers merely tightened about her arm as he led her down the stairs and across the hall into the living-room.

'Do you think she'll be all right?' she asked when they were no longer able to hear Sally's weeping.

'Graham Abbot brought Sally into this world,' Anton informed her in clipped tones. 'He's my neighbour, and he's an excellent doctor.'

This explained his quick arrival at Bellavista, but as time passed Laura's anxiety did not lessen. She accepted a cigarette from Anton and smoked it in agitated silence, but long after she had put it out there was still no sign of Dr Abbot.

'What's he doing up there that's taking up so much time?' she demanded eventually, glancing at the clock above the mantelshelf. 'It's been forty-five minutes!'

'Stop worrying,' Anton ordered, lighting his third cigarette. 'Sally's in good hands.'

'But what if——'

'Ah, here you are,' Dr Abbot's pleasant voice interrupted her, and they both swung round to face him as he entered the living-room.

'How is she?' Anton asked before Laura could formulate the words, and she was surprised at the hint of anxiety in his voice.

'She's quite calm now,' the doctor explained, placing his bag on the floor beside a chair and making himself comfortable. 'I've given her a light sedative, but it won't necessarily make her sleep.'

Relief swept through Laura, and, following the doctor's example, she lowered herself shakily into a chair.

'Graham, this is Sally's aunt, Laura Hoffmeyer,' Anton introduced her.

'Glad to know you, Miss Hoffmeyer,' Graham Abbot said absently. 'Most distressing business, the accident. Most distressing.'

'Could I pour you a drink, Graham?' Anton offered, turning towards the ornately carved oak cabinet in the corner.

Graham Abbot shook his grey head. 'No, thank you, but I suggest you pour one for yourself and for Miss Hoffmeyer. You're both going to need it before I'm finished with you.'

Laura's throat tightened in alarm, but it was Anton who said: 'That doesn't sound very good at all.'

'Depends on how you look at it,' the doctor shrugged thoughtfully.

A glass of wine was placed into Laura's hand, and Anton swallowed down a mouthful of his whisky before he seated himself in the vacant chair beside Laura's.

'Well, let's hear it,' he said abruptly.

Graham Abbot offered Anton a cigar, but Anton declined, and Laura watched nervously as the doctor rolled the cigar appreciatively between his fingers before he clipped off the end and lit it. 'There's nothing physically wrong with Sally, but we had quite a lengthy chat.'

'It lasted forty-five minutes,' Anton announced mockingly. 'Laura counted every second.'

Laura flashed him an angry glance, but the doctor continued speaking as if there had been no interruption.

'I don't think either of you realise what a shock it's been to Sally to lose both her parents at the same time,' he said, filling the room with the heavy aroma of his cigar. 'Heaven knows she didn't have much of a home life with Robert and Liz away most of the time, but she was happy enough, and now the only world she has known has been ripped from under her feet, so to speak. From her hysterical ramblings I gathered that she needs *you*, Anton, because you're familiar to the world she's known.' Graham Abbot paused momentarily, his grey glance resting on Laura as if he were summing her up for some or other reason. 'She needs you as well, Miss Hoffmeyer, because you're the only blood link she has left with her mother. There's no doubt in my mind that she's extremely fond of both you *and* Anton, and to part from either of you at this crucial time might unbalance her completely, I'm afraid.'

There was a brief, strained silence while they digested this news, then Anton asked, 'What do you suggest we do, Graham?'

Graham Abbot studied the ash on the tip of his cigar, and frowned. 'What you do is entirely up to yourselves, but I would like to add this last bit of advice.' He looked up then, and Laura felt an odd tightening about her chest which she could not explain to herself even if she tried. 'Sally is in desperate need of a stable home life, which is something she's never really known. It's my opinion that she needs the love and care of a mother *and* a father, and I suggest you both think very seriously about that.'

Another frightening little silence prevailed, and as she glanced quickly at Anton, Laura noticed that his eyes were narrowed to angry slits in his taut face.

'Do you realise what you're suggesting, Graham?' he demanded with a calmness that had an ominous ring to it, and Laura somehow did not dare to analyse the conversation.

'There comes a time in most people's lives when

they're forced to consider someone else's interests instead of their own,' Graham Abbot announced in that unperturbed fashion as he rose from his chair and picked up his medical bag. 'I'll call in again tomorrow.'

Seated alone in the living-room while Anton saw Graham Abbot to the door, Laura swallowed down a mouthful of her half-forgotten wine, and, as she felt the steadying warmth of the liquid surging into her veins, she drained her glass and placed it carefully on the low table beside her chair. She had the oddest feeling that something was about to happen; something which would affect her personal life, and when Anton finally re-entered the living-room, she was filled with an incredible wariness.

She refused his offer of another glass of wine, but she rose to her feet and stood about restlessly while she watched him pour a double whisky for himself.

'What are we going to do?' she asked with a feeling of trepidation spiralling through her.

'There's only one thing we can do, it seems,' he replied harshly, splashing soda into his glass. 'We shall have to provide her with the home she needs.'

Laura digested this carefully, rejecting several thoughts which leapt into her mind before she found the courage to ask, 'And how do you suppose we'll manage that?'

Anton swallowed down almost half his drink before he turned to face her, and there was a tightness about his ruthless mouth that made her quiver inwardly with something close to fear. He did not answer her at once, but his narrowed, piercing glance seemed to dissect her from head to toe where she stood waiting tensely for him to speak. She withstood his glance for what seemed an eternity, and then, when she had almost reached the limit of her endurance, he said tersely,

'You'll have to marry me.'

CHAPTER THREE

EACH tick of the clock on the mantelshelf sounded like the reverberating beat of a bass drum as Laura stared at Anton in stunned disbelief, but it was not the ticking of the clock she was listening to, she discovered at length, it was the thundering beat of her own frightened heart.

'You must be out of your mind!' she cried hoarsely, clutching at the back of a nearby chair when her trembling legs threatened to cave in beneath her. 'You can't seriously be suggesting marriage?'

His mouth twisted derisively. 'Can you think of a better solution?'

'There must be some other way to satisfy Sally's needs,' she argued in frantic desperation, refusing to accept the unthinkable solution he had suggested.

'If there was, do you think I wouldn't jump at it?' he demanded with a biting harshness that made her flinch, then he swallowed down the remainder of his drink and set his glass aside with a violence that nearly shattered it. 'Let's take the situation step by step. Sally needs a home with a mother and father thrown in for good measure. That immediately suggests placing her with foster-parents, but she also happens to need both you and me to the extent where it might unbalance her mentally to part from us.' He thrust his clenched fists into his pockets and strode towards the fireplace to stare broodingly down into the empty grate. 'Can you come up with a better solution than the one I've suggested?'

'I . . .' She shook her head in helpless confusion. 'No— but marriage is so—so binding.'

'Naturally it's binding,' he stated with remarkable tolerance as he turned to face her, but his eyes narrowed to slits of anger when he saw her frightened blue gaze resting on him. 'Dammit, Laura, do you think I want this any more than you do? I enjoy my life the way it is without a wife to clutter up the place, but, as Graham suggested, we should forget about ourselves and consider Sally's happiness instead.'

'Do you mean to say that Dr Abbot was actually suggesting marriage when he passed that remark?' Laura asked incredulously, unable to believe that anyone in their right mind would suggest marriage between two people who were almost complete strangers to each other.

'Indirectly, yes,' Anton replied tersely. 'When Robert asked me to be Sally's guardian, I agreed, but I never imagined that I would one day be needed in that capacity. I find it a nuisance, quite frankly, but she's my responsibility now, and I intend to do the best I can for her.'

'Even to the extent of marrying someone you don't— don't care for?' she asked haltingly, his resolute expression driving the remaining colour from her cheeks to leave her white and shaken.

'Yes,' he admitted with a determination that chilled her blood in her veins. 'As you pointed out earlier, Sally is nearing the age where she'll need the advice and guidance of a woman, and that's where you come in.'

'I see,' she murmured, her lips so stiff that she had found difficulty in moving them. She tried telling herself that she was living through a nightmare from which she would soon awaken, but she knew despairingly that this was not so.

'There's another reason, of course, why it might be wise for you to marry me,' Anton continued blandly. 'Graham warned me that people have begun to speculate about your presence here in my home.'

Laura felt the blood surge painfully back into her cheeks. 'You mean they think——'

'That you've not only slept under my roof, but in my

bed,' he finished for her with characteristic ruthlessness when she faltered with embarrassment.

'But that's ridiculous!' she protested angrily.

'You and I know that,' he said, crossing the room to her side, 'but who will believe us?'

'But we haven't been alone. Sally has been here in the house with us,' Laura argued indignantly as she found herself staring a long way up at him.

'If you were an outsider, would you consider a child of ten as an adequate chaperon?' he asked with a hint of mockery in his deep-set eyes.

'I suppose not,' she admitted grudgingly, 'but nothing like that ever crossed my mind.'

'Not everyone possesses a mind as pure and chaste as yours,' he laughed harshly.

'Don't mock me!' she retorted angrily, her cheeks flaming once more. 'I value my reputation even if you don't value yours.'

The atmosphere between them was suddenly electrifying. 'What makes you think that I have a reputation?'

She turned away from him, unable to sustain his piercing glance, but determined not to be intimidated. 'People wouldn't have been so quick to jump to the wrong conclusion if you hadn't built up a reputation for yourself with women.'

'Laura, you're an attractive, healthy young woman in your mid-twenties, and despite the fact that I'm nearing forty, I'm still considered an active, virile man,' he assured her with that hint of mockery still present in his voice. 'Put two elements like that together in one house for any length of time, and people are bound to consider the outcome as inevitable.'

'Dear heaven!' she exclaimed, burying her hot face in her hands.

'Heaven comes later when you've given me an answer to my proposal,' he stated with harsh cynicism as he forced the issue.

She swung round to face him, an unconscious plea in her eyes, and cold fear clutching at her insides. 'I *can't* marry you!'

'Can't? Or won't?' he demanded, his mouth drawing into a hard, thin line as he stared down at her from his imposing height.

'I need time to think it over,' she hedged desperately.

He glanced at his wrist watch. 'I'll give you five minutes.'

'Five minutes?' she echoed, her voice croaking in despair. 'Do you realise that you're asking me to decide in five minutes about something which will affect the rest of my life?'

The unrelenting lines of his jaw hardened considerably. 'It shouldn't take you long to decide whether your own happiness is more important to you than Sally's.'

His words implied that she did not care as much about the child as she had wanted him to believe and, like well-aimed arrows, they struck her most vulnerable spot with an agonising accuracy.

'*Naturally* Sally's happiness is of importance to me,' she stated emphatically, choking back the futile tears which threatened to overwhelm her. 'I want her to have all the love and attention which I've always felt Elizabeth had denied her by being away from her so often, and I want to see Sally grow into a healthy-minded young woman, but——' She faltered and gestured helplessly, pleadingly, but Anton was like an immovable concrete wall. 'Anton ... what kind of a marriage do you imagine it will be when we've entered into it for these reasons?'

'A healthy, normal marriage.'

Laura swallowed convulsively. 'You mean——'

'A sham marriage would never convince Sally of its security and stability, and I don't intend spending the rest of my life sharing my home with a woman who denies me access to her bed.' The colour came and went in her cheeks at the crudeness of his statement, but Anton seemed quite unperturbed as he glanced at his watch, almost as if he were concluding a business deal. 'Your five minutes are up.'

'Is there absolutely no other way?'

His eyes, like flints of steel, raked her mercilessly. 'You know the answer to that question as well as I do.'

Laura closed her eyes and leaned heavily against the back of the chair with her hands while her mind, like a computer, accepted and rejected every avenue of escape she could think of, until she was left with only one answer that mattered vitally. 'I would never forgive myself if I took my own happiness at Sally's expense.'

'Am I to understand, then, that you're agreeing to marry me?'

She raised her startled glance to his and, realising that she had sealed her fate by speaking her thoughts aloud, nodded slowly, her eyes filling with helpless tears as she resigned herself to the inevitable.

'Let's go upstairs and set Sally's mind at rest by telling her what we've decided.'

Laura felt certain that, had it not been for Anton's supporting hand beneath her elbow, she would not have managed to climb those shallow steps up to Sally's room where they found her propped up against the pillows, considerably calmer, but still wide awake, and she observed them warily as they approached her bed and seated themselves on either side of her.

Anton obviously did not believe in dilly-dallying and came straight to the point. 'What would you say if I told you that Laura has agreed to marry me, and that Bellavista will be your home in future?'

Sally looked from one to the other, her red-rimmed eyes wide and questioning in her pale face, but it was on Anton whom she finally fixed her intent gaze. 'You mean Aunty Laura won't be going away?'

'Just for a while, perhaps, to settle whatever she has to in Johannesburg,' he replied evenly. 'But we'll be married as soon as she returns.'

'Aunty Laura, is it true?' Dark eyes probed hers relentlessly for confirmation. 'You *will* come back? Promise?'

Just for one brief moment Laura shrank from replying. There was still time to change her mind, but once she had given Sally her promise there would be no turning back. She felt Anton's eyes on her, and saw the growing anxiety in Sally's glance, then her heart dictated the answer.

'I promise,' she whispered.

The change in the child's expression was so dramatic that Laura was left in no doubt about whether she had made the right decision.

'Oh, I think that's absolutely super!' Sally exclaimed exuberantly, leaping up from beneath the blankets to hug them both profusely. 'I'm so happy, happy, happy!'

'That's enough of that, young lady,' Anton ordered at last. 'It's time you went to sleep.'

Sally settled down obediently, but her eyes glowed with a new-found contentment as she looked up at them. 'Kiss me goodnight ... please.'

They complied with her wish, but Sally was not yet satisfied. 'Now kiss each other like Mummy and Daddy used to do to make the circle complete.'

'It will be a pleasure,' Anton replied, and before Laura could retreat in startled surprise, she felt his warm, strong fingers at the nape of her neck, and the hard pressure of his mouth against her own. The duration of that kiss was brief, but something had happened to her; something which she was still trying to define when he released her and turned his attention to the child who had observed them with obvious delight. 'Satisfied?' he asked with a faint smile.

'Yes,' Sally nodded happily. 'Goodnight.'

They put out the light and left the room, but when they stood facing each other in the dimly lit passage, Laura found that she could not look at Anton—not without her heart behaving in the oddest manner—and she kept her eyes firmly lowered to the wine-coloured carpet at her feet.

Her skin still tingled at the nape of her neck where his fingers had lain, and she could still feel the touch of his lips against her own. The memory of his kiss awakened sensations which she found difficult to analyse, but it sent a tell-tale warmth rushing into her cheeks.

'You'll become accustomed to my kisses,' Anton assured her mockingly as if he had read her thoughts, and her colour deepened, evoking his soft, deep-throated laughter.

Laura suddenly felt choked and horrifyingly close to tears. Her head was spinning in an effort to take in the events of that evening, and Anton's mocking remark had made her realise with shocking clarity that this nightmare was reality. For Sally's sake she had agreed to marry this autocratic man with the cold grey eyes and cruel mouth. For the rest of her life she would be at his mercy, and she shuddered at the thought of it.

Aware that Anton was observing her closely, she made an effort to control herself, and said quickly, 'I think I'd like to go to my room.'

'As you wish,' he nodded coolly. 'We have the weekend ahead of us to finalise our plans.'

If Laura had hoped to delay matters in some way, then she soon discovered that Anton had other plans. Within a matter of hours he had arranged, telephonically, for her to be released from her post as secretary to a firm of accountants and, through the Johannesburg branch of DeVere Enterprises, he found someone willing to take over the lease on her flat in Hillbrow. All that remained for Laura to do when she arrived in Johannesburg at the end of that week was to sell her furniture, settle her personal accounts, and pack her bags.

This was all accomplished with frightening speed, and within less than a week she found herself flying back to Cape Town in Anton's private jet. The black limousine was at the airport to meet her, with Eddie, the bulky helper, at the wheel, but it was the child who leapt from

the back of the car who caught and held Laura's attention.
Sally ran swiftly across the space dividing them and into
Laura's waiting arms.

'I missed you!' she cried and laughed simultaneously.
'I'm so glad you're back at last.'

'I missed you too,' Laura replied truthfully as she hugged the child close, but moments later she was glancing
about her nervously.

'Uncle Anton couldn't come,' Sally answered her un-
spoken question. 'He said he would see you at dinner this
evening.'

Irrational disappointment mingled with relief, but Laura
thought no more about it and, indeed, she was not given
the opportunity to dwell on the perturbing subject, for
Sally was hardly silent for one moment during the drive
from the airport to Bellavista.

Laura was amazed at the speed with which Sally had
overcome the shock of her parents' deaths, but then, of
course, Sally had been accustomed to not seeing Robert
and Elizabeth for lengthy periods of time, and this, Laura
supposed, helped tremendously to heal the pain of the
child's loss.

Bellavista was bathed in the warm glow of the late afternoon sun, giving the house and the surrounding landscape
that magical quality that nearly always succeeded in quickening her heart with appreciation. This was to be her home
in future, and although she could not deny the pleasure
this knowledge unwittingly aroused, there was another side
to it that filled her with secret dread.

Having to confront Anton at dinner that evening was an
ordeal she was not looking forward to. She knew that he
would wish to discuss the arrangements he had made with
regard to their marriage, but to her it was a subject that
did not bear thinking about. She delayed going down to
dinner that evening for as long as possible, but when Sally
marched into her room and announced, 'I'm hungry,'
Laura had no option but to accompany her down the

curved staircase with a sigh of resignation.

They passed the entrance to the dining hall which was used only for large, formal dinners, and a few moments later they entered the small dining-room which was used more often when not entertaining scores of visitors as it was situated conveniently close to the kitchen.

At their entrance Anton rose from his high-backed chair at the head of the table, and the wide breadth of his shoulders almost hid completely the heavy, gilt-framed portrait of one of his piratical ancestors who seemed to leer at Laura, with sinister intent, the moment they were seated.

An involuntary shiver coursed its way along her spine and, glancing covertly at Anton, she noticed for the first time his extraordinary likeness to the man in the portrait. The grey eyes beneath the heavy dark brows possessed that same piercing quality, and the features had been chiselled, as if by the same hand, into harsh, unrelenting lines, but Laura was more concerned at that moment as to how many of his ancestor's devilish characteristics Anton had inherited.

Anton poured wine from a crystal decanter into fragile, long-stemmed glasses while he made a few polite enquiries about her short stay in Johannesburg. She replied with an equal politeness, sipping at her wine to steady her nerves, and then the first course was served. An uncomfortable silence threatened, but Sally saved the situation by regaling them with an almost non-stop résumé of the class outing that morning to the historical Castle. Her incessant chatter appeared to irritate Anton, and Laura supposed she should have silenced the child, but she was grateful for the diversion, and stubbornly remained silent, allowing Sally to continue.

When coffee had been served, Anton was barely able to conceal his thunderous expression when he frowned down the length of the table at Sally. 'Isn't it time you went upstairs to bed?'

Sally wiped the traces of milk from her mouth with the

back of her hand, which further annoyed him, then her dark gaze went from Anton to Laura and back again as she remarked with astonishing shrewdness, 'I suppose you want to be alone.'

'You suppose correctly,' Anton replied, his expression forbidding any argument the child might have wished to enter into.

'Oh, well,' Sally shrugged reluctantly as she got up from the table, and, pouting a little sulkily, she said 'Goodnight' and went upstairs.

'Shall we go through to my study?' Anton suggested the moment they were alone. 'We shan't be disturbed there.'

In the book-lined study with its solid oak desk, leather chairs, and rugged stone fireplace, Laura felt as restless and uneasy as a hare with the hounds on its tail.

'What I have to say won't take long,' Anton assured her as he seated himself behind the desk and motioned her into a chair. 'We'll be married here tomorrow afternoon at three with Graham and his wife, Gina, as witnesses. They've also offered to take care of Sally while we spend the weekend at my Gordon's Bay cottage. We'll leave immediately after the ceremony, so have a suitcase packed and ready.'

'Do we have to go away?' Laura asked with difficulty, staring fixedly at the zebra-skin rug beneath her feet.

'It would look odd if we didn't.'

Her fingers curled nervously into the padded armrests of the chair. 'Anton, I ...'

Her throat dried up with fear. She tried again, but no sound came, and he interpreted her hesitation incorrectly.

'You want to change your mind?' he questioned her coldly. 'They say it's a woman's prerogative, but I call it fanciful unreliability. No woman can be trusted, or relied upon to keep her word.'

His cynicism moved her to an anger which loosened her tongue, and, rising jerkily to her feet, she said stiffly, 'It wasn't my intention to back out of our arrangement.'

He followed her example and rose to his feet, his height

placing her at a distinct disadvantage once again as he asked, 'Wasn't it?'

'No, it was not!' she argued hotly.

'Then let me guess,' he mocked her derisively. 'Like most women, you have expensive tastes, and you're disappointed at not having a white wedding with a lavish reception as you may have visualised. Is that it?'

'No!' she insisted sharply, but when she saw no glimmer of understanding in his coldly cynical glance, she turned away exasperatedly. 'Oh, you wouldn't understand!'

There was a tense little silence, then she felt him coming up behind her. 'Explain yourself.'

For a moment she could not speak as his nearness set every nerve in her body vibrating inexplicably, then she said dully, 'I—I think every girl dreams secretly of her wedding day. I imagined I would one day marry someone who would care for me as much as I cared for him, but instead I find myself marrying for coldbloodedly calculated reasons.' She shuddered inwardly. 'It all seems so wrong!'

His hands were on her shoulders, firm, strong, and relentless as he turned her to face him, but she could not raise her eyes higher than the knot in his grey tie.

'Our reasons for marrying each other may be calculated, but there's no reason for it to be coldblooded.' His arm was about her waist, a steel band imprisoning her against the hard length of his body and, startled by the unexpected swiftness of his actions, she stood helpless as he raised her face with his free hand and kissed her hard on the mouth. Resentment flared within her, but Anton seemed to anticipate her struggles, for his hand shifted its position to the nape of her neck, while his arm about her waist merely tightened like a vice. Her body grew taut with resistance, but he was obviously a man of experience, for he finally drew a response from her that left her trembling and breathless when she was at last released. 'See what I mean?' he smiled down at her mockingly.

Flushed and ashamed of the emotions he had aroused in

her, she asked coldly, 'May I go now, or was there something else you wanted to discuss with me?'

He inclined his head slightly. 'You may go.'

She felt his eyes boring into her back as she walked towards the door, and the hard, frantic beat of her heart did not subside until a few seconds later when she was crossing the hall towards the stairs.

The door between her bedroom and Sally's stood open, and when Laura approached it, the bedside light in Sally's room was snapped on.

'You should have been asleep ages ago,' Laura rebuked her gently, going into the room and seating herself on the bed beside the child.

'I'm too excited,' Sally announced, sitting up and hugging her knees.

'Excited?' Laura frowned.

'About tomorrow,' Sally explained, surprising Laura with her knowledge of the arrangements Anton had made. Those dark eyes glowed into Laura's as she asked, 'Aren't you excited, too?'

'Oh, Sally——' she began, but she felt so ridiculously close to tears that she choked back the rest of her sentence.

'What's the matter?' Sally wanted to know, the happy light in her eyes faltering.

Laura swallowed convulsively. 'Nothing—nothing at all.'

'You looked as though you were going to cry,' Sally insisted suspiciously.

Laura laughed shakily. 'I think I'm a little tired.'

'And frightened,' she could have added, but Sally would not have understood why anyone should feel afraid on the eve of their wedding.

'I think when I get married one day I'll be so excited that I won't be able to sleep a wink the night before,' Sally announced, happily quite unaware that Laura was thinking similar thoughts. She would not sleep a wink that night, but her sleeplessness would be as a result of fear, not excitement.

'Your wedding day is still a long way off, darling, and I pray that——'

'That what?' Sally prompted when Laura caught herself up in the act of saying that she hoped Sally would one day marry for love, and not out of duty.

'That you enjoy your carefree childhood while it lasts,' Laura substituted hastily, lifting the sheets for Sally to slide under, and tucking her in carefully before she dropped a light kiss on her cheek. 'Goodnight, sweetheart. Sleep well.'

She snapped off the light and returned to her own room, closing the interleading door so she would not disturb Sally while she bathed and prepared for bed.

The night was long and dark, and filled with frightening visions of a future shared with a man who was almost a complete stranger to her; a man who neither knew nor cared one iota for her feelings. After tomorrow's ceremony she would be his to do with as he pleased, and the thought filled her with such dread that she almost cried out into the darkness. She had had a brief taste of his mastery that evening; a mastery which had, admittedly, stirred her emotions, but which had also succeeded in making her aware of that streak of cruelty in him which had frightened her so often during their brief meetings in the past. He would take, giving nothing in return, and that, she felt certain, would be the basis of their marriage.

It was these disturbing thoughts that kept her awake until she could see the dawn sky through the lace at her window, then exhaustion claimed her, and she slept until Jemima woke her with a tray of breakfast shortly after eight.

'This is a happy day for us all, Miss Laura,' Jemima announced, her starched white apron crackling as she approached the bed and placed the tray on Laura's knees. 'I speak for everyone when I say that we wish you and Mr Anton happiness.'

'Thank you, Jemima,' Laura smiled, but, as the door closed behind the smiling woman, she wondered what happiness she could expect from a marriage perpetrated for the sole purpose of providing a home for her young niece.

The hours passed with alarming swiftness that morning. There was last-minute shopping to be done, and a wedding ring to select, and, through it all, Anton remained a remote, uncommunicative stranger in whose company she felt dreadfully ill at ease.

That afternoon, with time to spare before she went downstairs, Laura stared at herself in the mirror and decided that she neither looked nor felt anything remotely like a bride ought to on her wedding day. Her narrow-skirted dress with the lacy top was a rich, creamy colour instead of white, and, instead of joyous anticipation, there was fear and apprehension in the deep blue eyes that stared back at her.

A sharp tap on her door made her jump nervously, and she turned to face the door warily as it was pushed open a fraction.

'May I come in?' a bright, feminine voice enquired, and then, without waiting for a reply, a tall, attractive woman with dark, greying hair entered the room and closed the door firmly behind her. Her appraising glance took in Laura's confusion, and then she smiled with a warmth that melted some of the icy dread surrounding Laura's heart. 'We haven't met before,' she explained. 'I'm Georgina Abbot. My friends call me Gina, and my enemies dare to call me George.'

She wrinkled her nose in comical distaste, and Laura laughed for the first time in days. 'I'm certain you haven't any enemies.'

'You'd be surprised,' Gina remarked with a slight grimace, then she explained the reason for her presence in Laura's room. 'A girl shouldn't be alone at a time like this,' she stated emphatically, 'and while the men are indulging in those filthy cigars Graham always insists upon smoking, I thought that I would come up and keep you company.' There was a faint glimmer of uncertainty in the direct gaze of her green eyes as she asked, 'You don't mind, do you?'

'I don't mind at all,' Laura assured her at once, grateful for the presence of someone to talk to, but then a more pressing thought came to mind. 'Do you know where Sally is?'

'She's downstairs waiting anxiously to see you, but Anton has promised that she could come up and call you as soon as Mr Fuller has arrived.' Gina's critical glance took in Laura's appearance from her honey-brown hair, coiled in its usual knot at the nape of her neck, down to her cream and tan shoes. 'You look lovely, my dear,' she smiled warmly. 'Really lovely.'

'Thank you,' Laura smiled back nervously.

'Laura ...' Gina hesitated, then a look of determination flashed across her otherwise serene face. 'Do you mind if I sit down?'

'Please do,' Laura said hastily, drawing up a chair for Gina, and seating herself on the dressing-table stool.

'Laura, I know why you're marrying Anton,' Gina said now without hesitation, ignoring Laura's faint gasp of surprise as she continued. 'It couldn't have been an easy decision to make, but I admire you for it.' She leaned forward in her chair with a hint of urgency in her manner. 'Anton may be a hard man in many ways, and often quite ruthless when necessary, but he's also a man of great integrity. If you find him cynical about many things, most especially women, then you must forgive him, my dear. He was hurt very badly once, and he's never quite regained his faith in women.'

Laura stared at Gina for a moment, finding it difficult to believe that Anton DeVere had ever given his heart to a woman. She was only too aware that he possessed a virile masculinity and a sensuality of movement that would attract most women, and, according to the newspapers, there had been many women in his life, but none of them had remained long enough over the years for Laura to recall their names, let alone their appearances. Which one of those beauties, she wondered cynically, had succeeded in penetrating deep enough beneath that hard veneer to hurt him so badly?

'Why are you telling me this?' Laura asked curiously.

'Well ... firstly, because I happen to be fond of Anton, and I'd like to see this marriage succeed. Secondly, because the success of this marriage will depend largely on your patience and understanding, and thirdly,' she smiled humorously, 'because I think I'm going to enjoy having you as a friend and neighbour.'

A knock on the door ended their conversation abruptly, and an anxious little voice cried out, 'Aunty Laura, are you there?'

'Come in, Sally.'

The door was flung open and Sally almost stumbled into the room in her excitement, the pink, frilly dress enhancing the darkness of her eyes, and the sheen of her almost black hair hanging in two neat plaits down her back.

'Oh, you look beautiful!' she sighed, her eager glance taking in Laura's appearance, and then, remembering the purpose of her errand, she said excitedly, 'Uncle Anton says you may come down whenever you're ready. Mr Fuller has arrived and he's waiting downstairs.'

Laura nodded, her throat suddenly too dry to speak.

'We'll be down in a minute,' Gina intervened hurriedly, ushering the child from the room and returning swiftly to Laura's side.

'Gina!' Laura cried out her name in a moment of panic, gripping the hands extended towards her as if they offered safety from a danger as yet unknown.

'Courage, Laura, courage,' Gina whispered softly, her fingers tightening about Laura's, then she turned towards the door. 'Come down as soon as you're ready.'

Courage. She had never lacked courage before, Laura thought as the door closed behind Gina's slim, elegant figure in the blue and white suit. She had never before lacked the courage to face up to her convictions, but at this precise moment she felt the cowardly desire to run, and never to stop running until she was safe somewhere where Anton would never find her. This was the supreme test of her courage, she realised, and taking a deep, steadying breath, she cast a final critical glance at herself in the mirror before leaving her room and going downstairs.

In the living-room the Reverend Mr Fuller, Anton, and Graham and Gina Abbot awaited her arrival, and they turned to face her when she entered. 'Oh, God, what am I doing here?' she thought in a moment of blind panic as she paused just inside the doorway, and then she saw Sally, her eyes bright with excitement in her glowing, happy face. She had to go through with it for Sally's sake, she realised grimly, and she could only pray that she would find the courage to face what lay before her.

Anton stepped forward, his eyes narrowed and shuttered, and, as she placed her hand in his, she felt an inexplicable little shiver race through her. His mouth tightened, as if her hesitation angered him, then he drew her further into the living-room and the ceremony began.

CHAPTER FOUR

Mr Fuller, a portly gentleman with a red face, conducted the marriage ceremony in a voice that communicated its brittleness to Laura's nerves. A wedding ring, a cold, hard seal of possession, was slipped on to her finger, giving the man who placed it there the unquestionable right to her body, and at this thought she only barely succeeded in suppressing a shudder when Anton lowered his proud head to touch her lips briefly with his own when Mr Fuller made the customary suggestion that the groom should kiss the bride.

Champagne corks popped loudly, and glasses were filled in order to toast their happiness, but Laura felt a numbness shifting over her as if she had transgressed beyond the point of fear to a neutral plane where nothing, and no one, could touch her. The time to depart came all too soon. Graham and Gina kissed her as if they had known her for years, but it was Sally's clinging arms about her neck that registered most, and Laura caught her close in a rush of sudden warmth until Anton announced impatiently that it was time they left.

The white Jaguar purred down the long avenue of cypress trees, but, when Anton slowed down at the gate, a young man, camera in hand, leapt from the shrubbery. A light flashed blindingly, and Anton's muttered 'Damn!' seemed to explode in her ears. The next instant she was thrown back against the seat as he put his foot down on the accelerator and swung the car into the road with a violence that made the tires squeal. The Jaguar seemed to thrive on this unexpected burst of speed, but Laura, who had never been able to see the sense in risking one's life in this manner, was pale and shaken when Anton finally slowed down at the intersection several kilometres from Bellavista.

'Sorry about that,' he said abruptly, affording her just the briefest glance before they continued their journey at a more acceptable speed.

They arrived early enough at The Strand to pick up a few supplies, and then the final six-kilometre stretch to Gordon's Bay was accomplished within a matter of minutes.

The cottage was not exactly what Laura had expected, but it was nevertheless pleasing. An ivy creeper trailed along the whitewashed walls, and a small verandah offered an excellent view of the beach. The interior was sparsely, yet comfortably furnished, and while Anton carried in their supplies and suitcases, Laura opened the windows to alleviate the musty smell which had resulted from the cottage being shut up for a length of time.

It was an ideal retreat, she realised, for someone like Anton who obviously felt the need occasionally to escape from the pressure of his work.

Laura wandered into the first of the two bedrooms for a second time since her arrival, and her eyes inevitably strayed once more towards the old-fashioned four-poster bed. She swallowed convulsively, and fear returned with an intensity that forged a paralysing numbness into her limbs. With no chair available, she lowered herself gingerly on to the bed, and absently prodded the mattress.

'The springs don't creak,' a mocking voice informed her and, mortified, she leapt to her feet to see Anton placing their suitcases at the foot of the bed. 'You'll have to make up the bed yourself,' he added as he straightened. 'You'll find whatever you require in the passage cupboard.'

The sounds of the sea filtered pleasantly into the room through the open window, but Laura was aware of nothing else except her growing fear of this man who was now her husband. She must have been mad to contemplate a marriage such as this, she thought frantically as she met the direct gaze of those steel-grey eyes. There was no tenderness in his glance for the woman he had married that afternoon, only the cold, calculating hardness of a man summing up a newly acquired possession, and assessing its worth.

'Anton, would you——'

'Would I what?' he demanded when she faltered helplessly.

'Give me a little time,' she pleaded in a choked voice. 'Please?'

'How much time do you need?' he asked, his eyebrows rising sharply above those cold, heavy-lidded eyes. 'A month? A year, perhaps? Or do you need the rest of our lives?'

She shook her head and swallowed nervously. 'Only until we know each other a little better. Surely that's not asking too much?'

'I mean our marriage to start as I intend it to continue.'

'But, Anton——'

'No!' he interrupted harshly, closing the gap between them with one long, lithe stride. His hands were heavy on her shoulders, and her breathing felt oddly restricted when she felt his thumbs probing the sensitive hollows above her collarbone. 'It's a hurdle that must be crossed, Laura, and you won't find me an insensitive lover.'

'Don't!' she begged, suppressing a shudder at the intolerable thought of being possessed by him, but, at the same time, those caressing thumbs were sending a scintillating warmth flowing along her veins which was not entirely unpleasant.

'I'm your husband, Laura,' he was saying, 'and before this day has passed I'm going to be your lover.'

'No!'

'Accept it,' he stated harshly and emphatically, 'because that's how it will be.'

'You're inhuman!' she accused in a choked voice.

'Not inhuman,' he corrected, releasing her abruptly. 'Just practical.'

He strode from the room, leaving her alone and more

afraid than she had ever been before. There was no escape from this nightmare she had plunged herself into, and she would just have to see it through to the bitter end.

She collected the necessary linen from the cupboard in the passage, but hysterical laughter threatened to engulf her while she was making the bed. She felt like a condemned prisoner erecting her own scaffold before the hanging was to take place, and there was abject terror in her eyes when she eventually straightened from her task. She stared down at the wide bed, saw it as the battleground where she would suffer her most humiliating defeat, and wished suddenly that she were dead.

She prepared a meal for them that evening in the small kitchen, but found herself incapable of eating more than a mouthful, and when Anton finally suggested a walk on the beach, she jumped at the opportunity to delay the inevitable moment when she would be alone with him in the bedroom they were to share.

She had changed into a cotton frock and low-heeled sandals before dinner, but as they crossed the uneven sand Anton's hand was beneath her elbow, his touch warm, firm, and disturbing.

Stars clustered like diamonds in the night sky, and the ocean lay like a shimmering sheet of silver in the moonlight, but the beauty of it all escaped her as she walked stiffly at Anton's side, listening distractedly while he related to her a little of the history of Gordon's Bay. She heard nothing, however, beyond the fact that a Colonel Gordon of the Dutch East India Company had given his name to the bay when he had explored the southern coastline of Africa in 1778.

Anton's mocking, 'I don't seem to be making much impression as a tourist guide,' finally penetrated her panic-filled thoughts, and she blessed the darkness for hiding her discomfiture.

'I'm sorry,' she murmured apologetically.

'Shall we return to the cottage?'

'No! Not yet!' she wanted to cry out, but, with a submissiveness born of fear, she murmured, 'If you like.'

They strolled back to the cottage in silence, but it felt to Laura as if every step brought her closer to her doom, and she shivered uncontrollably when they finally entered the cottage and closed the door behind them.

Anton snapped on the light, but when her wide, frightened eyes looked up into his, he said harshly, 'I'll take another turn about the place before locking up.'

The outer door closed behind him with a decisive 'click' that made her flinch, but she felt a certain measure of relief as she hurriedly collected her things from the bedroom before going along to the bathroom at the end of the passage. She took her time bathing, but her heart lurched uncomfortably when she returned to the room and found Anton standing at the window with his back towards her. Her trembling hand automatically sought the wide neck-opening of her gown when he turned, but he merely stalked past her, removed his towelling robe off the hook behind the door where she had placed it, and continued on down the passage towards the bathroom.

She heard him in the shower while she removed the pins from her hair to let it cascade down on to her shoulders and, picking up her brush, she brushed her hair with long, firm strokes. The blessed normality of this nightly ritual seemed to steady her nerves temporarily, but, at the sound of the bathroom door opening, she realised that she was still as tightly strung as a bow, and ready to snap at the merest touch.

She lowered the brush on to the dresser as Anton entered the room, and her throat felt choked and dry when she turned to face him. His hair was damp from his shower, and as her stricken glance swept down to his bare feet, she felt terrifyingly certain that his muscular body was clad in nothing except that dark-blue towelling robe which left a large section of his deeply-tanned chest bare. She stared fixedly at the short dark hair curling against his skin, but when he came towards her she backed away instinctively, her heart leaping into her throat.

He paused abruptly, and his autocratic features contorted with something close to rage. 'For God's sake, don't look at me like that!'

'How do you expect me to look at you?' she demanded, forcing the words past the paralysing grip which fear had on her throat.

'I'm not a monster, Laura.'

'What you're expecting of me is monstrous,' she countered swiftly, her nervous fingers automatically tightening the belt of her gown.

'What are you afraid of, Laura?' His compelling eyes held hers captive as he lessened the space between them, and she stared back hypnotically. 'Are you afraid of the possibility that you might enjoy being made love to?'

'I shall hate every minute of it,' she hissed at him, but a disbelieving smile curved his mouth when he observed her heightened colour.

'We shall see about that,' he said with a strange emotion.

She stood immobile, caught between a weird kind of fascination and horror as he brushed aside her hands to undo the belt of her gown before sliding it from her shoulders to lie at her feet. The transparency of her nightdress offered her very little protection from the intrusion of his smouldering glance and, heated with embarrassment, she cried out hoarsely, 'You can't do this to me!'

His reply was to pull her against him, and with his hand in her trailing hair, he pulled her head back to expose her throat. His face became a twisted blur when her eyes filled with tears, then he lowered his head, and his lips trailed fire across her skin before that hard mouth fastened on to hers.

Laura fought against him with every ounce of strength she possessed, but the all-consuming passion of his kiss drained her of her resistance, and left her humiliatingly supine in his arms as he carried her across the room and lowered her on to the bed. His mouth never left hers as he snapped off the light to plunge the room into merciful darkness, then she felt him shrug himself out of his robe, but when he lay down beside her, her alarming suspicions were confirmed. There was nothing between them save the fragile thinness of her nightdress, and this, too, he was removing with a dexterity born of experience.

Her dulled mind came alive once more to what was happening, and her fear returned with every thundering beat of her heart until, submerged in a well of panic, she fought him off like someone demented, but there was no escape from the brute strength of a man intent upon satisfying his desire.

'Stop fighting me, Laura,' he ordered harshly, placing a muscled leg across her thighs to pin her thrashing body to the bed.

She flung every insult at him that she could think of, but he held her firmly until, exhausted, she had no strength left to fight off the sensuality of his lips and hands invading her body with an intimacy which had, till that moment, been forbidden to other men, and her humiliation increased rapidly when she found that he was drawing an unwilling response from her.

She felt his weight above her, and her nails bit into the hard flesh of his shoulders as her body grew taut with resentment and fear. 'Please! I can't! Please, Anton!'

'Relax, dammit, or you might get hurt!' he warned thickly, but her tension merely increased with the realisation of what was about to happen, and the despairing knowledge that there was nothing she could do to ward it off.

Her cry of pain was stifled moments later beneath his lips when he took possession of her. She submitted passively, giving him no encouragement. She was conscious of nothing except his powerfully moving body, and a numbness that left her devoid of all feeling.

When Anton finally rolled away from her, she lay for a long time staring into the darkness, dry-eyed and disillusioned. If this was what making love was all about, then she could do very nicely without it in future, she decided unhappily.

Anton stirred beside her. 'It wasn't my intention to hurt you, Laura, but you have only yourself to blame for what happened.'

'I hate you!' she hissed at him, and all the anger and humiliation she had suffered at his hands was locked up in those three words.

'Good,' he retaliated harshly. 'Hate from you is preferable to indifference, and I don't ever want my intelligence insulted by the use of the word "love" between us.'

'Love is a word you'll never hear from me, Anton DeVere, have no fear of that!'

'I'm glad we understand each other,' he said abruptly and, turning over on to his side, he promptly went to sleep.

She drew the sheets closer about her, and stared at his broad back while she tried to unravel her puzzling thoughts. They had just made the word 'love' taboo between them, and although she felt certain that she could never love him, it left her with a feeling of inexplicable sadness. What had happened, she wondered, that he should have turned his back so completely on love? Was it a defensive attitude against being hurt again, or did he simply have no love to give?

The latter seemed the most probable, but she did not dwell on the thought for long, for the sound of the surf lulled her into a deep but troubled sleep, and she became enmeshed in dreams fraught with sinister encounters. She finally sought refuge in the shelter of protective arms; arms that offered unquestionable safety and security and, sighing contentedly, she slept on dreamlessly until the first light of dawn stretched rosy fingers across the sky.

She stirred, opening her eyes lazily and, to her dismay, discovered that she had been lying in Anton's arm with her head pillowed on his shoulder. For one paralysing moment she could not recall what she was doing there, then the memory of her pain and disillusionment returned, and with it came the humiliating realisation that it had been *his* arms in which she had sought refuge from her dreams.

She had to get away, she thought frantically. She could not face him so soon after what had happened last night, but as she shifted her position carefully, trying not to wake him, a heavy arm was flung about her waist, and a mocking voice demanded in her ear, 'What's the rush?'

Her heart leapt wildly into her throat, almost choking off the sound of her voice as she said, 'I want to get dressed.'

His lips brushed against her ear, sending a little shiver through her that was intensified when his hand came up to clasp her breast possessively. 'I think I like you better as you are.'

'Go to hell!' she cried angrily, fighting off his lips and hands, and the unfamiliar sensations they aroused.

'It's heaven I shall be going to, Laura,' he laughed softly against her lips as he pinned her flailing arms at her sides, 'and this time I intend taking you there with me.'

'No ... don't!' she begged frantically, her body taut at the suggestion of renewed pain, then her lips were parted beneath the bruising pressure of his hard mouth.

A blanket of fear enveloped her mind, and it was some time before she made the startling discovery that his caressing hands were having a soothing effect on her, and, as the tension eased from her body, her skin began to tingle as if a thousand little nerves had suddenly come alive to his touch. He continued to caress her, taking his time until his experience must have told him of her receptiveness, then his lips and hands sought intimacies she no longer had the strength or the desire to refuse. He was arousing emotions within her which she had never imagined existed, and this time, when he took possession of her, she found it so intensely pleasurable that she clung to him in unashamed and rapturous delight, giving of herself freely until she was plummeted into a vortex of ecstatic fulfilment.

Spent, they lay beside each other, and for a time Laura was conscious of nothing except the thudding of her heart and an exquisite feeling of well-being, then Anton spoiled it all by raising himself up on one elbow to say tauntingly, 'I promised you a glimpse of heaven, didn't I?'

His mocking reference to the intimacy they had shared seemed to belittle an experience which she had considered almost sacred, and as she came down to earth with a thud, she heard herself ask coldly, 'Do you usually gloat over your triumphs in this manner?'

His faintly cynical smile deepened. 'If I'm gloating, then it's because I've made an intriguing discovery about you.'

'Have you?' she asked warily, drawing the sheets up higher in order to hide her nakedness from his invading eyes, but her action merely evoked his mocking laughter, and made her cheeks flare hotly with embarrassment.

'I've discovered that beneath that cool exterior of yours there lurks a passionate woman,' he told her, lowering his lips to her exposed throat where a pulse leapt in response to his touch. 'I think I'm going to enjoy being married to you, and teaching you all there is to know about the art of making love.'

Her body stiffened with distaste. 'Your experience is vast, no doubt?'

'I'm thirty-nine, Laura,' he stated calmly as he raised his head, and his mocking glance seared through her like a heated blade as he added, 'Had I been an inexperienced youth you wouldn't have found my lovemaking so enjoyable.'

Her cheeks grew hot with renewed humiliation and anger. 'Last night you——'

'Last night was different. You were tense and frightened, and hurting you was unavoidable.'

Laura stared up at him contemplatively. His dark hair,

so liberally flecked with grey, lay in an unruly fashion across his broad forehead, the deep-set grey eyes were razor-sharp and intent, and the lips which had kissed her with such practised sensuality were now drawn into a familiar hard line. She was seeing again the stranger she had married, instead of the man who had, moments ago, advanced beyond the barriers of her natural restraint to initiate her into a new and exciting world. Which was the real man? she wondered confusedly. The passionate lover, or this ruthless, mocking stranger?

She stirred eventually and sighed. 'I think I'd like to get up and get dressed, if you don't mind.'

'Certainly.'

He removed his arm from about her waist and leaned back against the pillows with his hands locked behind his head. Laura sat up, realised to her horror that she had nothing on, and realised, too, that she had to cross almost the entire length of the room to reach her nightdress where it had fallen on the floor the night before.

A quick glance over her shoulder told her that Anton was observing her with amused interest, and her anger erupted. 'You could at least have the decency to look the other way!'

'Why?' he demanded with an infuriating smile that fanned her anger. 'You're my wife, and after what we shared last night and this morning there's no part of your body that's not known to me.'

'You're detestable!' she flung at him across her shoulder.

'And you're beautiful when aroused in anger ... or passion.'

A choked cry escaped her as she darted across the room to retrieve her nightgown, but her mortification increased as she fled to the bathroom with the sound of his mocking laughter ringing in her ears.

He was a devil! she decided furiously as she ran her bathwater. A devil with no thought and no consideration for anyone but himself.

When she returned to the bedroom Anton had gone, but she found a note propped up against the mirror of the dresser, and it was addressed to her in his firm handwriting.

'When your temper has cooled sufficiently, join me on the beach for a swim before breakfast.'

'When my temper has cooled, indeed!' Laura muttered to herself indignantly and, with an agitated movement, she pulled the band from her hair to let it fall to her shoulders.

Typically, his note had been an order, not a request, and she would have been tempted to ignore it if she had not glanced through the open window to see the ocean sparkling so invitingly in the rays of the rising sun.

She went down to the beach a few minutes later wearing a short towelling robe over her swimsuit. Anton sat smoking a cigarette with his back resting against a rock, but when she approached he pushed his cigarette into the sand, and rose to his feet.

'I suggest we have our swim while we still have the beach to ourselves,' he said, unintentionally making it easier for her to face him by addressing a spot somewhere above her head.

Without a word she dropped her towel on the sand beside his and slipped out of her robe. She followed him at a running pace into the sea with her hair flying loose about her shoulders, and when the frothy breakers about her legs made her lose her balance, she gasped as her body struck the icy water. After a few moments she found the water exhilarating and swam about lazily, her body rising and falling in the swell of the sea. Anton swam a little distance from her, seemingly oblivious of her presence, and she felt quite startled when she found herself trying to decide whether or not she liked his inattentive attitude.

Laura had a vague suspicion that she disliked the idea of being ignored by him and, after a reasonable period had elapsed, she swam towards the beach and walked across the sand to where she had left her towel. She dried herself and rubbed her hair vigorously before spreading out her towel and seating herself comfortably with her back against the large rock. Taking her sun-glasses from the pocket of her robe, she pushed them on to her nose, and tried to forget for a time her disturbing thoughts concerning Anton's behaviour.

Gordon's Bay lay in a natural cove at the foot of the Hottentots Holland mountains, and although the sun-drenched beach was inclined to be rocky, it was apparently a fisherman's paradise, she realised as she watched two men reeling in their catch from the rocks some distance away.

A movement to her left drew her attention and, turning her head, her pulse leapt a little wildly. Tall and tanned, and with his wet hair plastered to his head, Anton was emerging from the sea. The water glistened on his muscled body, and a curious weakness invaded her limbs at the memory of the physical closeness they had shared.

She observed him covertly from behind the darkened lenses as he picked up his towel and dried himself, but she found herself staring at a remote stranger; a man who possessed her body, but not her soul. *Never* her soul! she decided grimly. She would make certain of that!

Anton lit a cigarette and sat down beside her, but once again she had that feeling that he could not care less whether she was there or not. She could not imagine why she should feel hurt about it, but she did, and, gathering up her things, she muttered some excuse for returning to the cottage, arriving there a few minutes later in a blind fury which was directed mainly at herself.

Anton continued to treat her in the same manner he had always done, and if, during that day, she succeeded in ridding her memory of the intimacy they had shared, then she could very easily imagine that they were not married at all. His customary cool politeness had never troubled her before, but now it stung painfully to be treated like a stranger, and that evening, when she joined him on the verandah after dinner, she could no longer deny the inexplicable yearning she felt for his touch. She despised herself for it, but she felt powerless to do anything about it.

She sat beside him on the bench, aware of him with every fibre of her treacherous being as they watched the incandescent moon climb higher in the starlit sky. The sound of the surf mingled with the chirping of the insects in the undergrowth as she and Anton talked quietly, but their conversation remained impersonal and dissatisfying, and she was finally driven to excuse herself for fear of making a complete fool of herself by displaying her feelings.

She went to bed, hoping to be asleep when Anton came in, but instead she found herself waiting, almost willing him to come to her.

'Damn!' she muttered angrily, thumping the pillow and turning on to her side so that she faced the window instead of the door.

How could she ever hope to understand him if she was all at once so incapable of understanding herself? She was behaving like a wanton, she told herself fiercely, and, burying her hot cheeks in the pillow, she finally went to sleep.

Laura awoke some time later to the discovery that the room was in darkness, and that she was being caressed with a freedom that made her blush.

'Anton?' she questioned unsteadily.

'Who else?' he demanded mockingly, and then her lips were parted with a deliberate sensuality that made her senses whirl.

She tried to resist this onslaught on her emotions, but her languorous body had a will of its own and responded to his touch with an eagerness she would no doubt be ashamed of later. Anton's lips left hers to seek the rounded softness of her breast, and at this point she became a slave to the desire that raced like fire through her veins. No longer aware of what she was doing, she locked her hands behind his head, and her body arched towards his in rapturous surrender.

'You've wanted this all day, haven't you?' he mocked her, but she had progressed beyond the stage where anything mattered except the passionate intensity of her emotions.

Later, as she lay awake beside him, his words rushed back at her with the force of the unrelenting ocean, and she was overcome with an acute sense of shame that made her feel as though she were blushing from the roots of her hair right down to her toes.

It was the truth; she *had* wanted him, and she could not have denied it even if she had been sufficiently coherent to do so at the time, but no one except Anton would have chosen a moment when she was at her most vulnerable to taunt her with the emotions he had so cleverly aroused in her. He was a heartless, ruthless devil, this man she had married, and heaven only knew how she was going to survive a lifetime of living with him.

They left Gordon's Bay the following afternoon to return to Bellavista, to Sally, and to the full realisation of what Laura would have to endure as Anton's wife. Their marriage had become the subject of tremendous interest, and often unkind speculation, and although they shared the same bed, she came no closer to understanding the enigmatic man she had married. During the first month of her marriage she discovered that she had been added to the long list of his many possessions to become something he could amuse himself with when he was not jetting across the country on business, and she resented this fact bitterly.

She discovered, too, that she was pestered by reporters wherever she went, and was subjected to a barrage of personal questions ranging from her marriage to Anton, to the death of her sister and brother-in-law. Her silence merely encouraged further speculation, and she eventually became petrified to the point where she seldom went anywhere without Anton for adequate protection.

The only one who seemed to be entirely happy with the situation was Sally. She adapted to life at Bellavista like a fish to water, totally content in the knowledge that Laura would always be there even if Anton was so often away on business.

On Anton's instructions, and despite the excellent bus service to and from Constantia, Eddie acted as chauffeur-cum-bodyguard to the unsuspecting child, and he not only drove her to school in the mornings but fetched her there in the afternoons as well.

Laura found herself left with plenty of time on her hands, and very little else to do except brood about what had become of her life and the dreams she had once nurtured of falling in love. She could not think of Bellavista as home, and neither could she adapt to the fact that she had taken up permanent residence in this magnificent city which was steeped in history from the time Van Riebeeck and his party had set foot on its shores. Perhaps, if things had been different, she would have settled more swiftly, but the unusual circumstances of her marriage had made it impossible for her to feel anything but an intruder. She blamed Anton's attitude for this, and although she did not want to think of him too often, she could not forget that he somehow had the power to arouse her to a degree of passion she had never imagined possible. But she could not love him. *Never!* He was ruthless and cynical, and seemed to take a diabolical pleasure in humiliating her when she lay in his arms, aflame with desire, and utterly vulnerable. She despised him for it, but she despised herself more for her own inability to resist him at such moments.

There was nothing strange in sitting down to an evening meal in the small dining-room with only Sally for company, and that evening was no exception. She listened to what Sally had to say about her school projects, and questioned her about her studies, and later, when Sally had gone up to bed, Laura indulged in her favourite pastime of weaving stories around Anton's piratical ancestor whose portrait hung against the wall facing her.

'You're always staring at old Friedrich DeVere's portrait, Miss Laura,' Jemima remarked humorously when she came in to clear the table.

Friedrich DeVere! So that was his name, Laura thought

excitedly and, pouring herself a second cup of coffee from the silver coffee pot, she said: 'Tell me about him, Jemima.'

'Friedrich DeVere was the first owner of Bellavista, but when he died his brother, Mr Anton's great-grandfather, took over the place,' Jemima informed her while she busily transferred the things from the table to the trolley.

'Is that all there is to tell about him?' Laura asked with curious disappointment.

'No, Miss Laura, but'—Jemima cast a nervous glance over her shoulder and added hurriedly—'Mr Anton won't like it if I talk about it.'

'Now you've *really* made me curious,' Laura laughed, adding milk and sugar to her coffee and stirring it quickly before she took a sip. 'Mr Anton isn't expected back until tomorrow, so tell me, please?'

Jemima hesitated, her nervousness quite apparent, but then she shrugged and launched into the lengthy explanation Laura had requested. 'Friedrich was a wild one, a fighter and a gambler. Some people called him the devil himself, but then he met a Miss Dora Goodchild soon after her arrival in South Africa, and fell in love with her. They say she was a refined and gentle lady, and Friedrich was like a lamb worshipping at her feet. The day before they were to be married she went for a walk up into the mountain. The mist came down unexpectedly, and she just disappeared.' Jemima shook her head sadly. 'Some people say she was buried under a rock-fall, and others say she was killed by a mountain lion.'

'And some people say that Friedrich still walks the mist at night searching the mountain slopes for the woman he loved,' a deep-throated voice spoke with unexpected sharpness behind them, making them jump guiltily.

'Mr Anton!' Jemima exclaimed, her dark eyes wide and filled with a nervous apprehension that matched Laura's as they both swung round to face the man who had entered the room so silently.

'You may go, Jemima,' he ordered abruptly, and the dishes rattled noisily as she hurriedly pushed the trolley from the room.

Laura had remained seated, however, a trickle of fear finding its way along her veins as Anton pulled out a chair and sat down close to her, but when she met his coldly penetrating glance she felt a renewed shiver of apprehension course its way up her spine.

'Don't blame Jemima,' she said in the woman's defence. 'It was I who pestered her for information.'

His mouth twisted into a cynical smile that did nothing to allay her fears. 'You're interested in my villainous ancestor?'

Laura swallowed down the nervous lump in her throat, and explained lamely, 'It's the likeness, I suppose, between Friedrich and yourself.'

'My grandfather always maintained that I'd inherited many of his villainous characteristics along with his looks.' His eyes mocked her ruthlessly. 'Do you agree?'

'I wouldn't know,' she said, making an effort to hide her discomfiture while she poured him a cup of coffee, but she felt his eyes, intense and hard, observing her, and her hand shook noticeably when she passed the cup to him across the table. 'What happened to him?' she asked hurriedly. 'To Friedrich, I mean?'

'When all attempts to find Dora failed, he shot himself,' came the harsh reply, and a derisive smile curved his lips at her shocked expression. He stirred his coffee and drank it down thirstily while she tried to digest this information, then he added savagely, 'The story of Friedrich and Dora has been romanticised out of all proportion over the years. If you ask me, she was stringing him along solely for the reason that she felt flattered to think that she could twist him round her little finger. It's quite likely that on the day she disappeared he discovered that she'd had a lover elsewhere. They quarrelled, and she walked out on him, it's as simple as that. Friedrich, like a fool, couldn't face the humiliation, and shot himself.'

'That's your version,' Laura concluded distastefully.

'That's my version,' he nodded with a distinct sneer about his hard mouth. 'And you must admit it's a damn sight more credible than the others you've heard.'

'I don't believe she walked out on him,' she argued for some unknown reason. 'I think something happened to her; something that prevented her from returning.'

'Such as a mountain lion dragging her up to its lair and devouring her?' Anton questioned, then he laughed disparagingly. 'That story is just as unlikely as the nonsense about Friedrich haunting the mountain on misty nights.'

'You're only saying that because you——' Laura bit back the rest of her sentence, horrified at how close she had come to revealing the information Gina had passed on to her on her wedding day.

'Go on,' he prompted, his eyes narrowed to angry slits. 'Because I what?'

Under the close scrutiny of his piercing glance she recovered herself swiftly and said the first probable thing that came to mind. 'Because, for some obscure reason, you prefer to have the worst possible opinion of all women.'

'My opinions were forced upon me by women such as Dora Goodchild,' he replied with a savagery that made her recoil from him inwardly. 'Prove to me that she didn't walk out on poor old Friedrich there, and you'll restore a great deal of my faith in women.'

Her anger flared suddenly. 'You know very well that I don't stand a chance of proving anything of the kind.'

'Exactly,' he stated harshly, rising to his feet. 'Now, I'm going up to shower and change, and then, I'm afraid, I have to go out again.' He leaned over her, the masculine scent of his body in her nostrils and, against her will, her senses were stirred. Strong fingers gripped her chin, and she found herself staring up into those hard, glittering eyes for interminable seconds before his mouth came down to crush hers in a ruthless kiss that left her lips bruised, yet tingling responsively. 'The subject of Friedrich will not be discussed again,' he stated decisively. 'Is that understood?'

Laura nodded silently, unable to speak even if he had demanded it, and then she was released to sit staring after him as he strode purposefully from the room. Her nerves settled back into their rightful order, but her eyes filled with tears when she glanced up to meet Friedrich's leering appraisal, and, for no apparent reason, she felt like weeping hysterically.

CHAPTER FIVE

LAURA had been asleep when Anton returned home late that evening, and when she awoke the following morning he had gone. Only the crumpled sheets, and the indentation left by his head on the pillows, indicated that he had slept beside her that night in that large bed with the intricate carvings in the heavy stinkwood headboard. She felt vaguely cheated by the knowledge that she had been unaware of his presence beside her in Bellavista's master bedroom, but she had no time to linger on the subject, and she washed and dressed hurriedly in order to see to it that Sally would have her breakfast and not be late for school.

'Did you ask Uncle Anton about going to Gordon's Bay for the holidays?' Sally asked expectantly when she got up from the breakfast table and picked up her school bag.

Laura smothered her feeling of guilt at having forgotten her niece's request, and shook her head. 'He was hardly home last night when he had to go out again,' she replied, thankful that this at least was the truth.

'We'll ask him this evening, then,' Sally stated firmly, hugging Laura briefly before running off to where Eddie's bulky figure stood leaning against the bonnet of the long black limousine with the DeVere family crest on its doors.

Through the window Laura saw Eddie smile and salute respectfully as he took Sally's bag and helped her into the back seat, and moments later the car disappeared down the long, sweeping drive. Laura could no longer hear the car's engine, and during the ensuing silence she became acutely conscious of her growing loneliness, and a longing for—she knew not what. Sighing heavily, she poured herself a second cup of coffee, and swallowed it down quickly, but, in the process of returning her empty cup to the saucer, her glance inevitably travelled down the length of the table, almost as if she expected to see Friedrich's portrait hanging against the cool white wall. Drawn as if by an unseen magnet, she left the breakfast-room and walked quickly down the passage towards the dining-room. There it was, Friedrich's portrait against the panelled wall, and, seating herself at the end of the table, Laura stared at it with a deep frown of concentration creasing her forehead.

The devil was in his eyes this morning, mocking and taunting her, and, quite suddenly, it was as if she were staring into Anton's eyes. They were coldly penetrating eyes; eyes that never displayed a fraction of warmth—not even when they were making love. There was desire, yes, but nothing more, and she shuddered at the memory of the times she had lain with his hard body against her own, hating him for the violent emotions he always succeeded in awakening in her, and despising herself for her inability to suppress her own desires.

Last night he had slept beside her without so much as touching her, proving conclusively, as he had done so often during the past weeks, that he could take her or leave her with equal unconcern. She was a plaything he could pick up, or discard at will, and the knowledge hurt like a fiery sword being driven into her very soul. His male independence had not suffered as a result of their marriage, and she imagined that he came and went very much the same as he had always done, but somehow he had succeeded in binding her to him with chains which were as strong as they were invisible. She was like a bird with clipped wings, fluttering in his hands until his will had subdued her, and then, his desire for amusement satisfied, she would be set aside and forgotten until the next time. She hated him! Oh, God, how she *hated* him!

'Miss Laura?'

She came to her senses suddenly to find Jemima staring at her curiously. She felt the cold dampness of perspiration on her forehead, and her hands were clenched so tightly on the table that her nails were biting into the soft flesh of her palms.

'Are you all right, Miss Laura?' the woman questioned anxiously, her dark eyes taking in the pallor of Laura's cheeks, and the shadows beneath eyes which had a faintly haunted look about them.

'I'm fine,' Laura managed with a forced smile as she pushed back her chair and stood up, but she turned away hastily when her lips began to tremble. 'I think I'll go for a walk in the garden. I need some fresh air.'

She left the house through the side entrance and walked briskly but aimlessly through the enormous grounds. She was being stifled slowly but surely in that house with its antiques and its unhappy memories of the past. Anton's forceful presence lingered in every room as well, like an unseen shadow reaching out to engulf her, and she wanted to escape, to flee from his domination of her mind and her body, but where could she go without taking with her that feeling of guilt at having to leave Sally behind. The child needed her; needed to know that she would be there when she returned home from school in the afternoons, and heaven knew Laura could never do anything to hurt a child who had been hurt so badly already.

A dove called to its mate in the tree above her, and the sound was strangely soothing, making her shiver involuntarily as the tension uncoiled within her. Deep inside her a little voice warned her to take care, or she might find herself being hurt far more than she had ever dreamed of. Hurt by whom, or by what? she wondered curiously, but the answer evaded her like the disappearing mist on the mountain slope which was forbidden territory at Bellavista.

Laura returned to the house eventually and slipped into the daily routine she had planned for herself, not giving herself time to think until she could help Sally with her studying when she returned from school that afternoon, and then the hours passed swiftly until it was time to sit down to the dinner she had planned that morning with Jemima.

Sally lingered at the table that evening after dinner, and she cast a quick glance in Laura's direction before she turned to Anton and said: 'The school closes on Friday for the Easter holidays.'

'So it does,' Anton replied evenly, pushing aside his cup and lighting a cigarette. 'Do you have anything special in mind for the holidays?'

'Could we go to your cottage at Gordon's Bay, Uncle Anton?' Sally asked with a pathetic eagerness that touched Laura's heart.

'I'll arrange for Eddie to drive you and Laura there on Friday afternoon.'

'Oh, but——' Sally's face clouded. 'But I want you to come as well.'

'I'm afraid that's out of the question,' Anton announced with bruising abruptness. 'I'm far too busy at the moment.'

'But, Uncle Anton——' Sally paused and glanced beseechingly at Laura. 'Tell him, Aunty Laura. He'll listen to you. Tell him it won't be any fun without him.'

'Forget it,' Anton snapped before Laura could open her mouth. 'I can't get away at this moment.'

Sally cast a bewildered glance from Laura back to Anton. 'But——'

'That's enough, Sally,' he ordered sharply, and the child's lips quivered.

'Oh, very well. I just thought——' Sally paused hopefully, but when Anton maintained an adamant silence, she got up from the table and said unhappily, 'I'm going up to my room.'

Steel-grey eyes captured Laura's glance as Sally left the room, and she knew instinctively that this was not the moment to pursue the subject. She drank her coffee quickly and excused herself, but when she left the dining-room she felt those cold eyes boring into her back.

A few minutes later she knocked briefly on Sally's bedroom door and entered without waiting for a reply. Sally was lying on her bed staring darkly up at the ceiling with her hands locked behind her head, and Laura closed the door softly behind her before she crossed the room towards the bed.

'May I sit down?' she smiled tentatively.

'I suppose so,' Sally muttered, making room for her on the bed beside her.

'Oh, come on, darling, don't look so glum about it,' Laura insisted in a lighthearted attempt to shake the child out of her mood. 'You and I could still have a lot of fun together, couldn't we?'

'I know that, Aunty Laura, but——' Sally removed her hands from behind her head and sat up, her lips curling petulantly. 'It would have been so much fun with Uncle Anton there as well.'

'I'll talk to him again, Sally, but I can't promise anything.'

Dark eyes regarded Laura intently. 'Will you really talk to him about it?'

'Yes, but——' Laura hesitated, not wanting to push her hopes up too high. 'If he really can't make it, Sally, will you promise to accept his decision?'

Sally considered this for a moment, and then nodded. 'I'll be disappointed, but I'll accept it.'

'Good girl,' Laura smiled, pinching the soft cheek affectionately between her fingers. 'Now, stop looking so unhappy, or you'll have me believing my company isn't good enough for you.'

'That's not true, Aunty Laura. I just love you to bits,' Sally exclaimed, and demonstrated this by flinging her arms about Laura's neck and hugging her effusively.

'And I feel the same about you, darling,' Laura assured her sincerely as she hugged the child against her and smoothed the dark head with a gentle hand. 'I think it's time you had your bath and went to bed, don't you?'

'Yes, Aunty Laura.'

Laura kissed her goodnight and prepared to leave, but Sally's voice halted her when she had opened the door, and Laura turned to face her unsuspectingly. 'Yes, darling?'

Brown eyes surveyed her intently across the room. 'You do love Uncle Anton, don't you?'

Momentarily taken aback, Laura stared at her, then she pulled herself together with an effort and, as convincingly as possible, she said: 'Of course I do.'

Sally frowned and fingered one of her long plaits. 'You never show it.'

'Your aunt and I aren't demonstrative by nature,' a voice said behind Laura, and her cheeks flared hotly as she swung round to see Anton standing there, but he barely glanced at her as he added, 'If you want a demonstration, however, I'm sure we could oblige you.'

Before Laura could utter a syllable in protest, she found herself draped across a muscled arm, and a hard mouth was pressed against hers in an impersonal, yet shattering kiss that left her clinging to him in a dazed fashion when he finally raised his head and glanced at Sally who had been observing them closely. 'Satisfied?'

'Yes,' the child nodded happily. 'Goodnight.'

Moments later, in the privacy of their bedroom, Laura turned on Anton angrily. 'That display was unnecessary.'

'On the contrary, I thought it extremely necessary for Sally's peace of mind. Besides ...' a humourless smile curved his mouth, 'you enjoyed it.'

A wave of hot colour surged into her cheeks and, swinging away from him, she said furiously, 'I loathed it, and you damn well know it!'

He followed her into the bathroom with long, angry strides, and she shrank against the rose-coloured tiles as he towered over her menacingly before her shoulders were taken in a bone-crushing grip. Her cry of pain was stifled when he pulled her up against him with a force which temporarily robbed her of breath, then feather-light kisses tantalised her lips until, with a shuddering moan, they parted to offer him the sweetness within. His hands left her shoulders to move down the length of her back to her hips in a possessively sweeping caress, and her treacherous body went limp against him as a sensual fire was lit within her. Her hands crept up his broad chest to become locked behind his strong neck, but at this point he drew back, and his taunting laughter penetrated her drugged senses to fill her with such intense shame and self-disgust that she cringed from him as well as her inner self.

'If that was a demonstration of your loathing, then loathe me all you want,' he continued to taunt her, his eyes like lasers burning into hers until it felt as though her very soul was being scorched.

She fell away from him to lean against the tiled wall, the quick rise and fall of her breasts beneath the silk of her blouse indicating her distress, and then the colour drained slowly from her face to leave her paper-white. The room swayed about her momentarily, but just as quickly it righted itself, and, closing her eyes tightly to shut out his twisted, cynical features, she whispered brokenly, 'Leave me alone, please.'

She would not have been surprised if he had ignored her request, but a few moments later she heard the bathroom door close, and when she opened her eyes again, she was alone.

A leisurely, scented bath did much to restore her equilibrium, but it did nothing for the deep-seated ache in the region of her heart. During those brief moments, while the room had swayed about her, she had discovered the reason why she had feared Anton ever since their first meeting on Robert's yacht. Physically, Anton had made a shattering impact on her senses, and something must have warned her, even then, that her heart would not escape unscathed if she should be foolish enough to tangle with him. With Robert and Elizabeth no longer there, fate had taken over in the cruellest way, and she had been thrust into the very hands she had wanted to evade. She could not put a label to her feelings—not yet—but she knew, without doubt, that the day would soon come when she would have to admit that Anton DeVere meant more to her than any man ever could or would in future.

She sighed unsteadily as she slipped her arms into the sleeves of her blue satin dressing gown, and she tied the belt firmly about her slim waist before leaving the bathroom. Relieved to find the bedroom empty, she seated herself in front of the dressing-table mirror to remove the pins from her hair. Long, firm strokes with the brush blended a sheen of honey into the soft brown, making her look young and vulnerable, and somehow appealing when Anton entered the room a few minutes later.

Her wide blue eyes took in his appearance from the sheen of dampness on his dark hair after his shower, down to the brown towelling robe which accentuated the superb physical fitness of his wide-shouldered, lean-hipped frame, and her heart hammered against her ribs as he came towards her. She was on the verge of panic when she noticed that he was carrying two mugs on a tray, and her questioning glance swept upwards once more to meet his.

'It's cocoa,' he told her abruptly with the faintest smile touching his lips as he placed the tray on the dressing-table and pulled up a chair for himself before handing her a mug.

Laura murmured her thanks unsteadily and frowned down into the cocoa as if the reason for this thoughtful gesture lay hidden in its milky depths.

'I haven't slipped poison into your drink, if that's what you're thinking,' he mocked her, and a flush stained her cheeks as she looked up sharply.

'I was thinking,' she told him coldly, 'that it was kind of you to make us something to drink.'

'It was thirst, not kindness, that made me do it,' he stated flatly, leaning forward to place a heavy hand on her knee. 'I'm never kind, and well you know it.'

She stared down at his hand in a hypnotic fashion, unable to move when he slid it up along her thigh in a sensually arousing caress that made her quiver responsively before he released her and sat back in his chair to drink his cocoa.

There had been nothing casual about his touch. It had been a deliberately taunting gesture to prove to her that he controlled her as completely as he controlled everything else in his life, but, for the first time, this thought did not repel her.

She felt his eyes on her while she sipped at her drink, and cursed herself for not having put on something beneath her gown. After almost two months of marriage to Anton she did not have to be told that his tanned, muscular body was clad in nothing but his towelling robe, and her cheeks went pink at the thought.

'Is there no possibility of your going with us to Gordon's Bay?' she asked hurriedly, attempting to steer her thoughts along a less disturbing avenue.

'No possibility at all.'

'But couldn't you——'

'Dammit, Laura,' he interrupted bitingly, placing his empty mug on the tray with a thump that made her flinch visibly as he got to his feet, 'I'm up to my ears in work, and you sit there nagging like a child!'

'I wasn't nagging,' she insisted calmly. 'I merely asked if——'

'I know damn well what you asked, and I've told you before that it's impossible at the moment.'

'We're supposed to be a family, you know.'

A tense silence followed her quietly spoken remark, and he turned to face her with barely concealed anger in the taut line of his jaw.

'Are you suggesting that I'm shirking my responsibilities?' he demanded with a dangerous calm that sent a shiver up her spine, but she sustained his glance unflinchingly.

'I'm not suggesting anything of the kind, Anton, but you

have been away rather more than you've been home during the past weeks.'

His eyes narrowed, and that hateful cynicism curved his hard mouth. 'Are you pleading Sally's cause or your own?'

Laura's back went stiff with resentment and anger, and she rose to her feet jerkily to place her mug on the tray beside his. 'You know very well that Sally has been looking forward to spending this holiday at your cottage, and her plans have included you.'

'And you, Laura?' he mocked her. 'Did *your* plans include me as well?'

'I don't give a damn what you do!' she lied, turning her back on him for fear of what he might see in her eyes, but Anton reacted swiftly, and steely fingers snaked about her wrist, swinging her about roughly to face him.

'I think you *do* give a damn!' he said through his teeth, his eyes glinting steel-like down into hers.

'Let me go!' she cried, attempting to free her hand, but succeeding only in having the other captured as well as he dragged her up against him and rendered her helpless by pinning her wrists behind her back.

The hard contact of his body against her own, and the clean male scent of him, attacked her senses like the affect of a drug, but as she threw her head back to glare up at him, he lowered his lips to her exposed neck to explore the sensitive column of her throat where every nerve and pulse quivered responsively.

'I've had the distinct feeling lately that, each time I've been away, you've welcomed my return with a certain eagerness.'

'Only your egotistical mind could think up something so absurd,' she argued, shutting her eyes in her desperate effort to fight against the tremors of delight that rippled through her.

'Is it so absurd to think that you miss my lovemaking when I'm away?'

'It's more than absurd,' she contradicted his taunting remark. 'It's ludicrous! I hate you to touch me!'

He raised his head suddenly and something in his eyes made her renew her frantic efforts to escape, but he merely laughed that cruel, harsh laugh while he gripped both her wrists in one large hand, leaving his other hand free to brush aside the wide collar of her gown to expose one smooth shoulder.

'Is it hate that makes you tremble when I touch you like this?' he asked mockingly, the deep timbre of his voice thrilling her while his warm hand moved in a sensually arousing caress from her shoulder to her breast, and despite her efforts to keep a tight rein on her emotions, she could not prevent her limbs from weakening against him as a shudder of ecstasy shook through her to prove, humiliatingly, how effortlessly he could arouse her emotions.

'Anton, please!' she begged, but her heart was beating so fast that it was an effort to speak. 'For God's sake, don't do this to me!'

'Is it hate that lights the fire of your passion until you cling to me and beg me to take you?' he demanded ruthlessly, ignoring her pleas, and fully aware of the sexual excitement he aroused within her while he undid the sash of her nightdress to gain access to the rest of her pulsating body.

'I've never yet begged you to maul me the way you do,' she protested, fighting him with every mental weapon she could find, but she shrank inwardly from the stinging fury of his glance.

'You don't know what it's like to be mauled by a man, but, by heaven, if you don't guard your tongue, I'll show you tonight!'

'I despise you!' she hissed frantically, but the next moment a cry was torn from her lips as, with one sweeping movement, he stripped her nightdress from her trembling body and raised her high in his arms. 'Let me go, or I'll——'

'Or you will what?' he interrupted with a harsh laugh,

his razor-sharp eyes raking her from head to foot before he
flung her on to the bed and followed her down to crush her
softness with the hard length of his body. Against her throat
he demanded, 'Are you going to shout for help so that
Sally can rush in to witness your inevitable surrender to my
lovemaking?'

She sucked her breath in sharply, a deep flush staining
her cheeks. 'You're detestable!'

'I find nothing more detestable than a liar,' he said cut-
tingly, and then his hard mouth was bruising her lips into
quivering submission. Laura fought him off with what
little strength she still had left, but her struggles merely
increased his desire for her, and when he finally raised his
head, the brilliant blaze of his eyes confirmed this. 'You
know very well that at this moment you want me so much
that you're aching with the same need that's tearing away
at my guts,' he accused thickly, and the devastating truth of
it made her renew her struggles, but her flailing arms were
grasped painfully at the wrists and raised above her head to
render her harmless. 'Deny it,' his deep voice grated along
tender, quivering nerves, 'and I'll have the satisfaction of
proving you a liar.'

She turned her hot cheek into the pillow and a low moan
escaped her as his lips and tongue explored the soft swell
of her breasts. She clung desperately to her sanity, but,
when his mouth finally fastened on to hers with a searing
passion that seemed to set fire to her soul, she melted
against him, and her hands, freed from his restraining
clasp, sought the opening of his robe and moved hungrily
across the warm, hair-roughened chest towards the broad
shoulders where the hard muscles rippled beneath her
caressing fingers. He groaned against her lips, his body
now hard and tense with desire as he caressed her with a
new urgency, and her flesh responded wildly to the intimacies of his touch. Desire leapt like a red-hot fire through
her veins and, no longer in control of her actions, she
wrapped her arms about his neck while her body arched

towards his with an aching need for closer contact.

Anton raised his head suddenly, breaking her grip, and the eyes boring down into hers challenged and mocked simultaneously. 'Can you still deny that you want me?' Her eyes, dark and stormy with the extent of her emotions, gave him his answer, and a smile of triumph touched his mouth. 'You can't deny it, and you know it.'

'You're a self-opinionated, arrogant swine, and I hate you!' she accused hoarsely when he released her and stood up to remove his robe.

He was supremely confident, and in no hurry to return to her while she lay there staring up at him, her honey-brown hair in disarray across the pillows, and her breath coming quick and unevenly across her swollen, parted lips as her hungry glance swept down the length of his tall, evenly-tanned, muscular body. She had become an alien to herself, torn between love and hate, despising herself, yet wanting him with every fibre of her being. She held out her arms to him impatiently, not caring that her action proved his dominance over her, and he came to her then, his heated flesh against her own exciting her beyond reason. He stretched out a hand to switch off the bedside light, and then, in the velvety darkness, he proceeded to prove his dominance over her once and for all.

She was tormented with feather-light, unhurried caresses until the bone-snapping tension of her desire made her do exactly what she had denied so fiercely before. She clung to him and begged urgently, 'Take me! Please, take me!'

His hard, thrusting body showed her no mercy after that, and they made love in a fury of passion that left her limp and exhausted, but utterly fulfilled.

For the first time since their marriage, Anton did not thrust her from him with an exclamation of disgust on his lips, and she lay in his arms, her love for him a pulsating, living thing between them as he held her gently and caressed her in the tender aftermath of their lovemaking. He nuzzled her ear and, with a contented sigh, she turned

fully into his arms, burying her lips against his warm throat
where she could feel the throbbing, rhythmic beat of his
pulse.

'Won't you change your mind and come with us to
Gordon's Bay on Friday?' she asked innocently a considerable time later, but the moment the words were
spoken she was made to realise her mistake.

Anton's fingers bit into her flesh as he thrust her from
him, and his voice lashed her painfully. 'Women are all the
same. They use their bodies to get what they want, but
that strategy won't succeed with me.' His hands were hard
on her body, inflicting pain where moments before they
had given pleasure, and his breath was ragged and harsh as
he moulded her to him. 'What I want from you I will take
when and how I please, and you'll get nothing in return.'

Shocked and startled by the suddenness of his attack,
Laura was forced to submit to the demands he made on
her. In the fury that raged through him he was deaf to her
pleas while he violated her body without the slightest consideration for her feelings, and when it was over, she lay
cold and shivering on her side of the bed, bruised in body
and spirit.

To use her body as a persuasive element had never occurred to her, but Anton was filled with such bitter hatred
and suspicion that he would never believe anything else of
her. What kind of women had he associated with in the
past? she wondered, choking back a sob. What kind of
woman would use her body as a weapon of influence to
satisfy a grasping nature?

Laura lay for hours nursing the ache in her heart, torturing herself with her thoughts while Anton slept, seemingly without a care, and it was almost dawn before she
herself drifted into an exhausted sleep.

She awoke with a start some hours later to find Jemima
beside her with a tray of breakfast in her hands.

'What time is it?' she asked, yawning sleepily as she
gathered the sheets closer about her while she shifted up
into a sitting position against the pillows.

'Almost nine o'clock, Miss Laura. Mr Anton said I was not to wake you earlier.'

Anton! His name jarred an unpleasant, best-forgotten memory, and Laura winced inwardly as Jemima placed the tray on her knees and left the room.

A bulky envelope addressed to her in Anton's bold black handwriting stared up at her from the tray, and she tore open the flap with trembling fingers to extract a single sheet of paper which was accompanied by a bunch of keys.

'Laura,' the letter began bluntly, 'Let last night be a lesson to you. I was initiated into a woman's treachery at a very early age, and no woman will ever have the pleasure of using her physical attributes to bend my will to hers. Try it again, and the consequences will be far worse than you've already experienced.

'I'm flying to Johannesburg this morning on business, and don't expect to return before Saturday. Eddie has been instructed to drive Sally and yourself out to Gordon's Bay on Friday afternoon, and I'm enclosing the keys to the cottage.'

His name, in firm arrogant strokes, adorned the bottom of the page, and, typically, there was no apology for his behaviour, only a warning which, after last night's brutality, she would be well advised to heed.

She had no appetite, and barely touched the breakfast which had been prepared with such care. She settled finally for a strong cup of aromatic coffee before she pushed aside the tray and went through to the bathroom to run her bathwater. An hour later she was climbing through a gap in the privet hedge at the side of the house, and making her way through the garden up to Gina Abbot's house with a light of determination in her eyes.

If anyone could tell her something about Anton, then Gina could, and Laura had every intention of finding out all there was to know about the man she had married, and most especially the reason for his twisted attitude towards women.

'Am I in time for tea?' she asked with forced brightness when she found Gina coming out on to the terrace with a tray, and saw her placing it on the cane table with the glass top.

'Laura!' Gina looked up in surprise. 'I must have known you would come,' she laughed, gesturing towards the extra cup on the tray. 'Sit down, my dear. It's been some time since your last visit.'

Laura sat down in the cane chair and glanced about her appreciatively, taking in the scarlet bougainvillaea ranking so profusely on the pergola beneath which they were seated. Sliding glass doors led the way into the spacious living-room which possessed a homely atmosphere despite its elegant furnishings, and Laura found herself relaxing now that she was away from the austerity she always encountered within Bellavista's walls.

'You have a lovely home,' she announced sincerely as she accepted a cup of tea from Gina, and helped herself to a biscuit.

Gina's green eyes sparkled humorously. 'Coming from the mistress of Bellavista, that's a compliment.'

'I still can't think of Bellavista as my home,' Laura confessed, admitting to herself silently that there were many occasions when she still had the distinct feeling that she was there on sufferance.

'Time will change that,' Gina assured her, then she diverted the conversation in a different direction. 'I suppose Sally is looking forward to the school holidays. Have you made any plans?'

'We're going to the cottage at Gordon's Bay,' Laura told her casually, choosing her words with care as she added, 'Sally and I tried to persuade Anton last night that he should come with us, but unfortunately he won't be able to manage it.'

'What a shame,' Gina frowned. 'Sally must be disappointed.'

'She is.'

'And you, Laura,' Gina prompted with a teasing sincerity. 'Are you disappointed?'

'For Sally's sake, yes,' Laura replied calmly, giving nothing away as she drank her tea quickly before launching into the subject which was foremost in her mind. 'On my wedding day, Gina, you said that Anton had once been hurt badly. Was it a woman?'

'I wondered when you'd ask,' Gina laughed mischievously, then she sobered. 'Yes, it was a woman— Camilla York her name was then. They were going to be married, so everyone believed, but before the engagement could be announced, she married a wealthy German count and left the country.'

'But why?'

'Why?' Gina smiled a little cynically. 'My dear, this happened eight years ago. Anton's father had just died leaving DeVere Enterprises at rock-bottom financially. Anton never mentioned the subject, but my guess is that Camilla got out quickly when she discovered that the DeVere fortune had taken a tumble. Karl von Dissel happened to be on the scene, and he was also extremely wealthy. Added to that he was titled, and that was obviously just up Camilla's street, as they say.'

Laura smiled a quick, humourless smile. 'You don't make her sound very nice.'

'She wasn't,' Gina insisted, her green eyes sparkling with an inner anger. 'And Anton was well rid of her. If she'd been worth her salt she would have stood by him during those first few years after his father's death. He worked like a demon to put the family business on its feet once again, and today it's one of the largest firms of its kind in the country. There's no longer any need for him to work so hard—he has highly qualified people at the helm of each department—but he goes on and on, driving himself harder than he drives those who work for him. Heaven only knows what he's trying to accomplish, but Graham says that Anton will drive himself into an early grave if he doesn't slow down.' She leaned forward anxiously in her chair. 'Will you try to reason with him, Laura? Make him realise what he's doing to himself?'

'Anton is a law unto himself,' Laura smiled ruefully. 'He's master of his ship, and ruler of his kingdom. He doesn't take kindly to interference, and my reasons are quite likely to be misconstrued.'

'I know,' Gina nodded, 'but keep in mind what I said and when the time is right, use whatever influence you have.' A warm smile flashed across her face. 'At the moment he may be rather blind where you're concerned, but in time he'll realise what a gem he has for a wife.'

'You always do a pretty good job of boosting my morale, Gina,' Laura laughed, but her laughter brought her close to tears. 'Thank you.'

Gina had shed some light on the subject of Anton's cynical attitude, but there had to be more to it than that, Laura decided when she returned to Bellavista later that morning. Upstairs in their bedroom she found Anton's letter and read it through once again. One sentence stood out above all the others: 'I was initiated into a woman's treachery at a very early age.'

'A very early age,' Laura repeated the words softly to herself. When he was a child, perhaps? Or could he have been referring to himself when he had been in his teens, a time when most people were inclined to be over-sensitive? Had there been someone else at the time? Someone Gina had no knowledge of?

Laura's compassionate heart ached for him, but her logical mind remained vaguely unsympathetic, reserving judgment until all the facts were known. Anton was not a fool. Surely he must know that not all women are as despicable as Camilla von Dissel, and goodness knows how many others there may have been who unwittingly attributed to his low opinion of women.

She lowered her eyes to the letter in her hands, and the first sentence sprang to life. 'Let last night be a lesson to you.' She winced at the memory of his cruelty. Last night had been a night of pleasure and pain, and the latter was something she hoped she would never have to endure again.

CHAPTER SIX

THE sun rose behind the Hottentots Holland mountains with a lazy brilliance, transforming the small coastal town into a breathtaking paradise of green hills reaching out into the sea, with a stretch of golden sand dividing them. It held Laura spellbound and reluctant to climb down from her comfortable perch on the rocks in order to return to the cottage.

This was their fourth day at Gordon's Bay, and although the days had passed swiftly with Sally as companion, Laura had spent the nights in a restless turmoil, wondering what Anton was doing, and torturing herself with the memory of that last night they had spent together before his flight to Johannesburg. Her inability to sleep had driven her from her bed each morning before dawn to await the sunrise on the rocky beach, and afterwards she would return to the cottage feeling oddly at peace with herself.

The breeze moved playfully through her hair, lifting it from her shoulders and blowing it against her cheeks. In her haste to leave the cottage that morning she had not bothered to pin it up, and she flicked it back absently now, turning her face into the breeze so that it lifted her hair gently in a thick honey-brown curtain behind her.

The sea was never still, rising and falling like a living, breathing thing sending foamy breakers rushing towards the shore. It lashed the rocks beneath her motionless figure, sending up a frothy spray that left crystal-coloured drops on her cheeks like lost tears beneath shadowed blue eyes. A seagull settled on a rock nearby, cocking its head in her direction as if expecting to be fed with titbits, but when none were forthcoming, it flapped its wings and flew off with a disgusted screech.

The sound of its departure made her stir. Sally would

soon be awake and wanting her breakfast before they went for an early morning swim, and Laura sighed inwardly, for after a hectic day, another sleepless night would follow.

'Don't move!' a voice ordered sharply when she was about to get to her feet and, startled into immobility, she obeyed until that same voice said a few seconds later, 'You can relax now.'

She turned her head swiftly and her cautious, yet curious glance encountered a tall, lanky man with untidy sunbleached hair. His denims were as faded as the blue shirt he wore, and the sandals on his feet had obviously seen several summers.

'May I know what all that was about?' she demanded, wary of strangers after some of the encounters she had had with reporters, but she could not prevent her lips from quivering in response to his flashing smile.

'My apologies,' he replied, moving a book in the air as he climbed over the rocks towards her. 'I couldn't resist sketching you. You looked like a mermaid sunning herself on the rocks.'

'You're an artist?'

'For my sins, yes,' he said, and white teeth flashed in a thin, hungry-looking face as he seated himself beside her without invitation. 'The name's Alex Muir.' He paused, grinning as he added hopefully, 'You may have heard of me?'

Laura gave the matter unnecessary thought, then she shook her head. 'Can't say that I have.'

'Ah, my ego has been mortally wounded, but no matter,' he laughed teasingly, then she was placed under the direct scrutiny of his remarkably alert hazel eyes. 'May I know your name?'

'It's Laura—Laura DeVere,' she added hastily, still finding it difficult to link her name with Anton's.

'DeVere,' he frowned thoughtfully. 'You're not related to *the* Anton DeVere of DeVere Enterprises by any chance, are you?'

Hearing Anton spoken of in such grandiose terms sent an unpleasant ripple of shock through her, making her see the situation from an angle which had not occurred to her before, but which was now intolerably clear. Anton was a prominent and wealthy businessman from one of the most distinguished families in the Cape, while she was a nobody from nowhere whose niece happened to be his ward—it was as simple as that! And nothing, not even marriage to him, could elevate her to a position where she might imagine herself worthy of him in any way.

She became aware of Alex Muir awaiting her reply, and said in a voice that sounded curiously flat to her ears, 'I'm his wife.'

A long, low whistle emanated from the lips of the man seated beside her as he studied her with renewed interest. 'Some men have all the luck!'

Laura felt her cheeks grow pink and got to her feet. 'I have to go.'

'Not yet.' Long, sensitive fingers curled about her wrist with surprising strength. 'Would you sit for me?'

'Sit for you?' she asked blankly, her mind too full of her own disturbing thoughts to grasp what he was referring to.

'I must do this portrait of you seated on the rocks,' he explained. 'I've done the preliminary sketches, but I'd like to do a more detailed portrait.'

Laura shrank from the idea, and freed her wrist from the grip of his fingers. 'I'm sorry, but I——'

'I shan't impose on too much of your time,' he interrupted persuasively, rising to his feet and looking incredibly tall because of his thinness. 'I have a studio in Cape Town, and my number is in the book.'

'Mr Muir, I don't——'

'Alex,' he corrected swiftly with that flashing, all-embracing smile which she was certain could charm a bee away from its honey at times. 'Everyone calls me Alex.'

'Very well, then ... Alex,' she relented, unable to suppress the answering smile that curved her lips. 'I'm afraid sitting for you is out of the question. I'm flattered, but—I don't think my husband would approve.'

'Can't say that I blame him for being jealous and possessive where you're concerned,' Alex replied, jumping to the wrong conclusion, but she did not correct him, and he shrugged lightly. 'Oh, well, I'm returning to Cape Town tomorrow. If you should change your mind, give me a ring some time.'

'I shan't change my mind.'

'I shan't give up hoping,' he assured her as she climbed off the rocks and leapt on to the sand. She turned to glance back at him contemplatively, and he raised his hand in salute. 'So long, mermaid.'

Mermaid. The word echoed through Laura's mind while she hurried across the soft golden sand towards the cottage, and she giggled suddenly, but it was a mirthless, faintly hysterical sound which she was forced to stifle when she entered the silent cottage to find Sally awake and dressed.

'Where have you been?' she demanded accusingly as she came down the passage towards Laura. 'I've been worried about you.'

'I'm sorry,' Laura replied, instantly contrite. 'I took a walk down to the beach, and lost track of the time while I sat on the rocks watching the sun rise.'

'I was worried,' Sally repeated, her eyes filling with sudden tears. 'I thought something had happened to you.'

'Oh, Sally!' Laura drew the child against her and held her tightly, understanding her fears. 'I shan't go out like that again without telling you, and that's a promise.' Sally's arms tightened convulsively about her waist and, lowering her head until her cheek rested on the smooth, dark head, Laura whispered, 'Come with me to my room so that I can do something about my hair, then you can tell me what you would like to have for breakfast.'

'Don't tie up your hair,' Sally said at once, drawing a little away from Laura to look up at her with serious brown eyes. 'You look soft and pretty with it hanging loose.'

Laura was not sure at all that she wanted to look soft and pretty, but if it pleased Sally at that moment, she would leave her hair down, and, taking the child's hand in hers, she led the way into the kitchen.

After breakfast that morning they tidied the cottage, went for a swim, and scoured the beach for non-existent shells. After lunch Laura drew the curtains and made herself comfortable on the spare bed in Sally's room, mainly to encourage the child to rest in the heat of the day, and later that afternoon they went down to the beach once more. Sally amused herself building sand-castles, and Laura finally became involved in her efforts, but the tide was coming in and, after the first wave demolished their carefully constructed castle, it turned into a hilarious game which had Sally rolling about helplessly each time a wave reduced her castles to untidy heaps of wet sand.

When Sally eventually tired of the game, Laura sat back on her heels and observed her closely for a moment before asking, 'You're not unhappy, are you, Sally?'

'Of course not,' Sally replied at once, a faraway look coming into her eyes. 'I miss Mummy and Daddy sometimes, but I'm happy staying with you and Uncle Anton.' She looked up at Laura suddenly, and sighed, 'I wish Uncle Anton were here with us now, don't you?'

'I wish it too,' Laura replied with a sincerity that came from a heart filled with a sudden longing to see Anton, to be near him, to touch him, and, suppressing a little sigh, she tugged playfully at Sally's hair. 'Let's have a quick swim before we return to the cottage to see to the dinner.'

The water was cool against her sun-heated skin, and they swam about vigorously, joining hands occasionally to plunge into the waves, and emerging a few seconds later, coughing and spluttering with laughter.

They surfaced on one such occasion and, when their laughter subsided, Sally wiped the water from her eyes and blinked, then she pointed towards the beach, and shrieked, 'Uncle Anton! It's Uncle Anton!'

Laura swung round in disbelief, then her heart lurched in her breast, and her legs felt as if they had suddenly turned to jelly. The man walking tall and erect across the almost deserted beach towards the spot where they had left their towels was unmistakably Anton, and Sally, wild with excitement, was running through the shallow water and up the sandy beach towards him, her wet pigtails flapping behind her. Laura followed at a slower pace, drawing a horrified breath as, with a total disregard for Anton's immaculate grey suit, Sally flung her wet body against him and locked her arms about his waist.

'Oh, to be a child!' she thought with sudden envy, but her envy turned to embarrassment when she realised that her appearance left much to be desired. Her hair hung in limp, wet strands about her face and shoulders, and Anton's keen glance wasted no time in roaming with systematic slowness down the length of her bikini-clad figure as she walked across the sand towards him with a fast beating heart.

'Hello, Laura,' he said casually, his face expressionless now as he raised his glance from her tanned, shapely limbs to observe the heightened colour in her cheeks. 'Surprised to see me?'

'Surprised isn't quite the word,' she replied in a remarkably controlled voice while she pulled on her beach robe and tied the belt firmly about her waist.

His hard mouth curved cynically. 'Disappointed, then?'

'Of course she's not disappointed,' Sally chimed in unexpectedly, and then, to Laura's mortification, she added, 'Aunty Laura has been wishing you were here just as much as I have. She said so this afternoon.'

'Did she now?' Anton remarked softly, and Laura felt herself go redder still beneath his gaze.

'You may kiss each other, if you like,' Sally announced, increasing Laura's embarrassment as she added with childish reassurance, 'I won't mind.'

Laura wished at that moment that she could dig herself

into the earth like a sand crab, never to come out again, but somehow she remained standing, her head held high, her cheeks flaming.

'I think not, young Sally,' Anton observed with a wry smile. 'Laura is shy.'

'You're not shy, are you, Aunty Laura?'

Laura stared down into those questioning brown eyes and changed the subject firmly. 'I think it's time for us to get out of these wet things and into something warmer.'

'You *are* shy,' Sally accused with a giggle when she noticed Laura's reddened cheeks. 'Mummy and Daddy were never shy. They were always kissing each other, and making love.'

Laura groaned inwardly and placed her cool hands against her hot cheeks while she searched for something to say, but it was Anton who brought the conversation to an end by saying abruptly, 'I think it's time we stopped chattering and went inside as your aunt suggested. There's a chill in the air, so come on.'

Laura showered and washed the sand out of her hair, and dried it thoroughly with her small electric drier before slipping into slacks and a warm cashmere sweater. Anton, too, had changed into something more comfortable, she noticed when she entered their bedroom. Green suede pants hugged his narrow hips tightly and accentuated the long length of his muscular thighs, while the cream-coloured knitted sweater clung to his broad shoulders and complimented his tanned complexion. His presence in the room unnerved her considerably, but she tried not to show it as she sat down in front of the mirror to brush her hair vigorously.

'Leave your hair down,' he said unexpectedly when she was about to twist it up into its customary knot, and when it fell down to her shoulders once more in a thick silky curtain, he came up behind her and pushed his fingers through it lightly. 'I like it this way,' he added, a faint smile hovering about his hard mouth.

Their eyes met in the mirror, and she trembled when she felt his warm fingers brushing against her skin at the nape of her neck. The last time those hands had touched her, they had inflicted pain, she recalled, but it was a memory she did not want to dwell on.

'What made you change your mind about coming here?' she risked questioning him.

He smiled again that cold, cynical smile she hated so much. 'I managed to get things done sooner than I expected.'

In the harsh light above the mirror his face looked drawn, and she saw for the first time the lines of fatigue beneath his eyes, and the deeper lines running from nose to jaw.

Compassion stirred within her breast, filling her with a tenderness she had never expected to feel for this hard, often cruel man, and she said with impulsive concern, 'You look tired.'

His hands left her hair, and his expression hardened, making her realise her mistake as he demanded, 'Is that another way of telling me I'm old?'

'Don't be silly,' she retorted angrily, rising to her feet and swinging round to face him. 'Don't always search for hidden meanings in everything I say.'

'A woman seldom says exactly what she means.'

'Don't judge me by the standards of the women you've known, Anton,' she snapped back at him.

A brief, stormy silence followed, then his lips curled in a sneer that made her wince inwardly. 'Do you consider yourself to be unique?'

'No,' she shook her head and swallowed nervously. 'Not unique, just ... different.'

'Different?' Those hard eyes raked her mercilessly from head to foot. 'No, Laura, you're no different from any other woman I've known. You're all liars and cheats, and a man who places his trust in a woman is a fool.'

'I'm not a liar, and I'm not a cheat, and I——' Indignation choked her. 'I consider your remarks insulting!'

'I wasn't insulting you, I was merely stating the bare facts,' he insisted, but she had heard enough and made for the door. He was there before she could reach it, kicking it shut with his foot and leaning his weight against it. 'Where do you think you're going?'

'Anywhere where I don't have to see you, or speak to you,' she retorted, her eyes blazing up at him in hurt and anger.

'Do you find the truth unpalatable?'

'Does it give you pleasure to make me pay for all the times you have had your faith destroyed in a woman?' she counter-questioned furiously, wishing she could strike him, but knowing that she would be the one to suffer afterwards.

'Did you know that your eyes are a deep sapphire blue when you're angry?'

Momentarily floored as she was by his remark, her reflexes were sluggish, and his hands were biting into her waist, drawing her against him before she could do anything to prevent it. Her palms were flat against his hard chest as she leaned away from him and hissed, 'Let me go, do you hear?'

'Not until you've welcomed me as a dutiful wife should,' he announced, unperturbed by her efforts to escape.

With one arm like a steel band about her waist, his free hand grasped a handful of her hair, and her head was forced back so that her neck was arched painfully. For a brief moment their glances were locked in silent battle, then his mouth descended on her with an unexpected yet familiar sensuality against which she had no defence prepared. Her resistance took a tumble, and she gave herself up to the soaring tide of emotion that swept through her as she felt his warm hands against her skin beneath her sweater. His fingers explored her breasts through the fine lace of her bra, and the sweet ecstasy of his touch made her senses swim in surrender. She had the satisfaction of feeling his heartbeat quicken beneath her hand, and then she was released to stand swaying with the force of her emotions.

'Just as well we waited till now,' he mocked her without mercy as he stepped away from the door. 'That was not the sort of welcome a child should witness, was it?'

Laura drew a shuddering breath as she fought to control herself, then she spat out angrily, 'You're insufferable!'

She wrenched open the door and stormed down the passage into the kitchen. She hated him with every breath in her body, she told herself fiercely, mentally strangling that persistent little voice which dared to contradict her at that moment.

Laura's anger had subsided considerably by the time they sat down to dinner that evening, but she was quite content for Sally to dominate the conversation, for it gave Laura the opportunity to observe Anton without him noticing.

That air of masculine virility which always surrounded him seldom made her notice the increasing number of silver threads in his dark hair, but she saw them now, and her throat ached suddenly. He *did* look tired, she thought, and silently she echoed Gina's sentiments that he drove himself too hard. Physically he must be one of the fittest men she had ever known, but the demands he made upon himself were sometimes frightening to observe.

He looked up unexpectedly and, caught in the act of staring, her face became suffused with colour. For several disturbing seconds she could not look away, but when he raised his eyebrows enquiringly, she hastily lowered her lashes and stacked their plates into the sink.

'When are you going to have a baby, Aunty Laura?' Sally demanded some minutes later, and Laura almost choked on a mouthful of hot coffee.

'Yes, Laura,' Anton added fuel to the fire, 'when *are* you going to have a baby?'

'I haven't given it a thought,' she admitted with a calmness she was far from experiencing as a hot wave of colour swept upwards from her throat into her face.

'Is it important that we have a baby?' Anton wanted to know, his amused attention directed at Sally.

'Most people have babies when they get married,' Sally announced, her eyes alight with excitement. 'Just think how much fun it will be! I could take it for walks in the garden, and I could help look after it when you go out.' She glanced anxiously at Laura. 'You will let me help you with the baby, won't you?'

'Of course she will,' Anton answered for Laura, clearly enjoying her discomfiture.

'You're both forgetting something,' Laura began tritely. 'I'm not going to have a baby.' She crossed her fingers under the table and looked everywhere but at Anton as she added decisively, 'Not yet, anyway.'

Anton observed her intently, but said nothing, and Sally looked positively crestfallen for a time until her agile mind leapt to a different topic of conversation. Laura breathed an inward sigh of relief, but the incident had unnerved her considerably.

Her marriage to Anton had not come about for the usual reasons, and although they were married in every sense of the word, the possibility of having a child had somehow never occurred to her. For a woman of her age she should have had more sense, she admonished herself, but then she could not blame only herself for their thoughtless behaviour.

Later that evening, when Sally was tucked up in bed, Laura went out for a breath of fresh air and found Anton leaning against the wooden rail on the verandah. He looked peculiarly lonely standing there in the darkness, and she experienced an inexplicable desire to rush out and fling her arms about him in a comforting, protective manner. The feeling was so strong that she hesitated on the doorstep, giving herself time to control herself, and to suppress her feelings before she joined him.

She almost laughed out loud at her naïveté a few minutes later when she sat quietly beside him on the wooden bench, smoking the cigarette he had offered her.

Anton would never need to turn to anyone, least of all herself, for comfort or protection of any kind. He was a self-contained man, she thought a little cynically, and he was fully capable of shaping his own destiny, as well as that of others.

She had found it peaceful on other occasions to sit there in the darkness with only the sound of the surf to disturb the silence, but tonight was different. She was conscious of Anton there beside her; conscious of a muscular thigh almost touching her own, and conscious, too, of his brooding surveillance.

He brought the silence to an end abruptly, and shattered her fragile composure by asking, 'Does the thought that you might have my child disgust you?'

'No, of course it doesn't,' she said at once, surprised and faintly irritated that he should wish to continue the discussion on this particularly disturbing subject. 'It's just that I'd never given it a thought before.'

'You should have,' he mocked her. 'We haven't exactly been doing anything to prevent it, have we?'

'N-no, I suppose not,' Laura was forced to admit, her cheeks stinging with embarrassment as she put out her cigarette and clenched her hands tightly in her lap. 'Do you particularly want children?'

'Not particularly, but I think it might be nice to have a son; someone who could take over from me when I'm no longer there.' He leaned towards her; his arm along the backrest behind her, and his thigh warm and hard against her own as he brought his lips close to her ear. 'Will you have a son for me, Laura?'

Laura felt curiously winded, and it was several seconds before she could speak. 'Children are supposed to be born out of two people's love for each other.'

'Love!' Anton snorted in disgust, the controlled violence in his voice making her flinch noticeably. 'My God, that word has been used so often it stinks of deceit!'

He had risen to his feet to stand with his hands clenching the wooden rail, and she followed him there with the overwhelming desire to shake sense into him. 'Anton, you can't——'

'Replace the word "love" with "sex", then you'll be nearer the truth,' he interrupted ruthlessly.

'No!'

At her cry of denial he swung round to face her, and even in the darkness she could feel his eyes boring into her. 'Define love for me.'

'It isn't possible to define it.'

'Because it doesn't exist!'

'Oh, Anton, how can you say that?' she sighed helplessly.

'I'm not blind to the truth,' he argued harshly, sweeping her into his arms with a swiftness that took her by surprise. 'This is the only thing that makes any real sense— holding a woman in my arms, and knowing the desire to possess her body.'

'And when that desire is no longer there?' Laura asked weakly when his hard mouth had left hers. 'What then?'

He released her abruptly and turned away to light a cigarette, the flame of his lighter illuminating his harsh features briefly before he spoke. 'When that desire is no longer there, I shall seek my pleasures elsewhere.'

He could not have hurt her more at that moment if he had struck her, but now, at least, she knew exactly where she stood—on unstable ground which could cave in beneath her at any time.

It was some time before she was capable of speech, and even then she was shaking so much that she had to clutch at the railing for support as she said coldly, 'One day, Anton, you'll know what it is to love someone, and I hope I'm around when that happens, because I shall then have the pleasure of laughing at your downfall.'

'You will never hear me confess to loving anyone,' Anton stated icily with his back turned rigidly towards her.

'I hope, for your sake, I don't,' she retorted stiffly, walking blindly into the cottage.

Anton followed her inside a few minutes later. She heard him in the shower, and she was brushing her hair with angry, vigorous strokes when he finally entered the room. She put down the brush with a jerky movement and, conscious of the transparency of her night attire, she turned her back on the intense scrutiny of his eyes. She felt too raw, too hurt to feel anything but contempt for him at that moment.

If he came near her she would scream, she told herself, but Anton came up behind her with the silent swiftness of a panther descending on its prey, and when his hands gripped her bare shoulders her quivering lips refused to utter a sound.

She remained rigid, determined not to give in to him, but already that warm sensuous mouth against her throat and shoulder was doing something to her she would have given anything to deny. The tip of his tongue flicked into her ear, and a shiver of unwanted delight swept through her, while the tantalising scent of his aftershave lotion filled her nostrils and stirred her senses. She tried to move away, to break the spell he was weaving about her, but his hands merely tightened on her shoulders, and moments later she was trapped in the web of her own devastating emotions.

Why fight it? she asked herself at length. Why not accept what he had to offer while the offer still lasted? To-morrow she might hate herself, but in years to come the memory of these shared moments might be all she would have to sustain her through life.

Her nightdress slithered to the floor at her feet, and coherent thought deserted her as those strong hands fondled her breasts. She leaned back against him weakly, her eyes closed, her lips parted on a low moan of ecstasy, and suddenly she was airborne, her arms locked about Anton's neck as he carried her towards the bed and lowered her on to it. He knelt over her, his hands planted firmly on either side of her body, and she saw his eyes fill with an intense hunger as they travelled over her, devouring her nakedness in a way he had never done before.

'God, Laura, you're beautiful,' he said thickly. 'Don't let me first have to break through the wall of your resistance. Give yourself to me tonight.'

She stared up at him through lowered lashes, veiling what lay hidden in her heart, but unable to deny the aching need within her, and she agreed silently to his demand, allowing her actions to speak for her.

Shyly at first, and then with growing confidence, she untied the belt of his robe, slipping her hands inside and moving them in a slow, bold caress across the wide expanse of his hair-roughened chest. His skin was warm beneath her palms, the muscles rippling beneath her exploring fingertips as he shrugged himself out of his robe and flung it from him impatiently. His eyes burned down into hers as if to probe the depths of her soul, then he lowered himself on to her with a groan and buried his face in the scented hollow between her breasts, a shudder of desire shaking throughout the length of his body. Above the thundering roar of her own heartbeats Laura heard him murmur her name in a voice quite unlike his own, and an odd feeling of triumph assailed her when he finally raised his head and sought her lips with his own.

They made love that night in a way they had never done before. They exchanged kisses and caresses, tenderly at first, and then with a growing urgency until they came together in an explosive union that rocketed them to ecstatically delirious heights.

Later, in the languorous aftermath of their lovemaking, Laura held Anton close and breathed a silent prayer that he would never tire of her. He might never love her as she loved him, but she would do everything within her power to keep the flame of his desire alight. If desire was all he had to offer her, then she would nurture it with tenderness and care.

CHAPTER SEVEN

LAURA slept dreamlessly that night for the first time since coming on holiday to Gordon's Bay, and she did not awake until the sun filtered in through the window the following morning. Anton was no longer in bed beside her, so she took a quick bath before changing into a cool summer frock and sandals.

She was still checking on her make-up when Anton walked into the room and closed the door behind him. Their eyes met in the mirror; hers questioning, a little shy, and his distinctly mocking. He brushed aside the thin strap of her dress with a lazy finger, and lowered his lips to the satiny smoothness of her shoulder before he drew her to her feet and kissed her with lingering intent on her quivering, responsive lips.

'Happy birthday.'

Laura surfaced swiftly. She had forgotten completely. In fact, she had never given it a thought, and, raising her startled, questioning glance to his, she asked: 'How did you know?'

'Your birth date happens to be on our marriage certificate, but who do you think sent you those telegrams on your birthday each year when Elizabeth was off somewhere with Robert on his yacht?'

'You sent them?' she gasped in dismay, and not quite sure how she felt about it. 'Elizabeth asked you to send them?'

'I offered the first time when she bewailed the fact that she would be unable to send you a telegram on your birthday, and after that I sent it off automatically each year whenever they were away,' Anton explained, and, releasing her, he said abruptly, 'Turn around. I have something for you.'

Stupefied, Laura obeyed, standing perfectly still while he gently brushed her hair out of the way and fastened a necklace about her throat. It was the most magnificent piece of jewellery she had ever seen, she thought dazedly as she stared at herself in the mirror and lightly fingered the delicate design in gold which was so richly studded with diamonds and blue sapphires.

'Anton ...' she began helplessly, so totally overwhelmed by his gift that words failed her as she turned to face him. 'What can I say?' she whispered finally.

He smiled faintly. 'Do you like it?'

'It's the most beautiful gift I've ever received,' she whispered, and, to her dismay, her eyes filled with tears.

He stared at her oddly and raised a hand to her face, brushing away the single tear that spilled over on to her cheek with his fingers. 'I've never known a woman to cry before when I've given her something.'

'You must think me stupid, but——' Tears of happiness and delight choked her and, grasping his strong wrist in both her hands, she turned her lips into his palm in a spontaneous gesture. 'Thank you.'

Seemingly astonished, he raised his heavy eyebrows sharply above those deep-set eyes, then he drew his hand from hers, and caught her against him in a fierce embrace which was painful yet pleasurable. The softness of her trembling mouth was crushed beneath his in a hard, satisfying kiss which left her clinging to him dizzily when he finally raised his head.

There was a sharp knock at the bedroom door, and Sally's voice demanded haughtily, 'Aren't we *ever* going to have breakfast this morning?'

'Just coming,' Laura assured her, and then a more pressing thought came to mind as she stood in the circle of Anton's arms and stared up at him solemnly. 'Anton, did you change your mind about coming because you remembered my birthday?'

His expression became shuttered, and with his lips

against her throat creating havoc with her emotions, he asked roughly, 'What difference does it make? I'm here, aren't I?'

'Aunty Laura?' Sally called sharply, bursting into the room impatiently, then she stopped dead in her tracks to survey them with wide, slightly indignant eyes. 'I thought you said that you weren't demon—demon——'

'Demonstrative?' Anton supplied the word she was searching for, ignoring Laura's attempts to wriggle free of his arms. 'It so happens that we aren't demonstrative in front of prying eyes such as yours,' he added smoothly, glancing at Sally sternly from his great height. 'We like our privacy, so next time you find yourself facing a closed door, young lady, you knock and wait until you're admitted.'

Sally's lips curled in a slightly petulant fashion before she lowered her eyes to the floor and muttered, 'Sorry.'

'And don't sulk,' Anton ordered before asking in a lighter tone, 'Are you hungry?'

'I'm starving!' Sally exclaimed, recovering swiftly.

'So am I,' Anton admitted and, taking Laura's hand, he drew her towards the door. 'Come on, let's have breakfast.'

A surprise awaited Laura when she entered the kitchen. Anton and Sally had prepared an enormous breakfast between them, and in her place at the table stood a small gift-wrapped parcel.

'Happy birthday,' Sally laughed excitedly, flinging herself at Laura and kissing her enthusiastically. 'Now open your present.'

Laura obediently undid the wrapping to find that her gift from Sally was a tin of her favourite body talc, and the ready tears returned to her eyes once more when she suspected that Anton had had a hand in this as well.

'You're a darling, Sally, and thank you,' she cried, hugging Sally tightly in her arms.

Over Sally's dark head Laura's eyes met Anton's, and her heart leapt with a crazy warmth when he smiled at her without a trace of his usual mockery. This was truly a birthday she would not forget in a hurry.

When the time came to return to Bellavista, Laura closed the cottage door behind her with a genuine feeling of regret. It had been a holiday to remember, and during those warm autumn days she had watched Anton unwind gradually, the lines of strain disappearing from his ruggedly handsome features to leave him relaxed and more approachable.

'I'm so glad you came, Uncle Anton,' Sally told him with childish sincerity when he had stacked their suitcases in the boot of the white Jaguar. 'It's been fun, and I'm so glad we're a family now.'

Laura's throat tightened, but, surprisingly, it was Anton who took Sally in his arms and said: 'I'm glad we're a family too.'

He stretched out a hand towards Laura, silently including her in his statement, and when his fingers closed about hers she felt a warmth enfolding her heart with an aching sweetness. Oh, God, she loved this man so much, and how very much she yearned to make her feelings known to him. Surely, if she loved him enough, he would eventually learn to love her in return?

'It's time we left,' Anton interrupted her thoughts, and later, as they sped towards Cape Town, the week the three of them had spent together at Gordon's Bay became a delightfully happy memory Laura would have reason to cling to desperately during the long, painful weeks ahead.

'Laura, how much does your marriage to Anton mean to you?' Gina asked unexpectedly one morning while they were having tea on Bellavista's wide sun-stoep.

'It ... means very much to me,' Laura replied cautiously, and a little surprised that Gina should ask.

'Do you love him?' Gina persisted, and when Laura hesitated, she gestured expressively with her hands. 'I'm sorry, my dear. I wouldn't normally pry into your affairs like this, but I do have a very good reason for asking,' she explained, repeating her query. 'Do you love Anton?'

Laura nodded, so accustomed to hiding her feelings that she was unable to confirm them verbally.

'Has he mentioned Camilla von Dissel at all recently?' Gina questioned her, and the mention of that name sent a tremor of inexplicable fear along Laura's nerves.

'Her name has never been mentioned between us,' she replied truthfully, but her mouth felt dry, and her stomach muscles seemed to be twisting themselves into a painful knot. 'Why do you ask, Gina?'

Gina's green glance was unwavering and filled with concern when it met Laura's. 'My dear, I think you should know that Camilla von Dissel arrived in Cape Town a few days ago. Her husband died some weeks ago leaving her a wealthy widow and, from what I'm told, she's returned to South Africa with her sights firmly set on Anton.'

Laura shivered as if an icy wind had blown against her skin. 'Surely she must know that he's married?'

'My dear Laura, a woman like Camilla would consider that no obstacle at all,' Gina laughed a little cynically. 'If she wants him, then she'll certainly do everything in her power to get him.'

'Anton wouldn't be fooled by her again,' Laura argued, not wanting to believe that Camilla von Dissel was capable of severing the still fragile bond which linked her in marriage to Anton.

'Men are silly creatures, really,' Gina remarked scathingly, 'and Anton wouldn't be the first man to make a fool of himself twice over the same woman.'

It was no use sticking her head in the sand like an ostrich, Laura realised at length. Camilla had once featured prominently in Anton's life and, if she was clever enough, she could do so again.

'Do you think he knows?' Laura asked anxiously. 'That she's back, I mean?'

'I'm certain he does.'

'You sound more than certain—you sound convinced.' Laura clenched the arms of her chair so tightly that her knuckles shone white through her skin. 'What is it, Gina? Have you been told something?'

'It isn't what I've been told, it's——' Gina paused and bit her lip as if she were angry with herself. 'It was nothing,' she ended in her most convincing manner, but Laura was not fooled for one moment.

'Please, Gina. I must know.'

Gina shifted uncomfortably in her chair, unable to meet Laura's eyes while she spoke. 'I met Graham in town yesterday. We had lunch together at that new Sea Point restaurant, and . . .'

'Anton and Camilla were there together,' Laura filled in for her when she paused uncertainly.

'Look, my dear,' Gina began with some urgency as she leaned towards Laura and placed a sympathetic hand on her arm. 'I'm fond of you, and so is Graham, or I wouldn't be here today talking to you like this. I'm not saying that you have reason to fear the worst, but forewarned is forearmed, they say, and Graham thought that I would be the best one to enlighten you.'

Laura was silent for a long time, trying to assimilate the information Gina had passed on to her, then she smiled stiffly and said: 'I'm grateful to you, Gina.'

This talk with Gina placed Laura on the alert, and she began to notice things she might have overlooked before. Anton began to miss dinner on countless evenings, arriving home late at night to occupy the bed in the dressing-room. It was, so he had said, not to disturb her with his late arrival at night, but Laura would not have been human if she did not begin to suspect that he was seeking his pleasure in the arms of the woman he had once loved so passionately.

She was torturing herself unnecessarily, she told herself firmly one morning when she drove herself to town in the small blue Mazda which Anton had given her. At twelve-thirty she telephoned his office on the spur of the moment, hoping to have lunch with him as she had done several times before, and hoping, at the same time, that his presence would alleviate her foolish fears, but his secretary informed her, with unsuspecting truthfulness, that he had gone to an early lunch with Countess von Dissel, and that he was not expected back before three that afternoon.

The most important thing at that moment was not to allow her imagination to run away with her, Laura told herself in an attempt to view the situation logically, but jealousy and suspicion coursed through her veins like a veld fire. Anton had always been a stickler as far as taking only an hour for lunch was concerned, but with Camilla von Dissel he suddenly relaxed that rule, stretching it to almost four hours. No one in their right mind lingered over lunch for four hours. What were they doing? Talking, perhaps? Making love?

'Oh, God!' she groaned when she reached the Mazda and dumped her parcels on the back seat before sliding wearily into the driver's seat. 'I must trust him,' she hissed at herself through clenched teeth. 'I must have faith. If anything good is to come out of this marriage, then I must believe in him. I *must*!'

'Believing in Anton is like believing that the storm clouds in the sky are nothing but candyfloss,' a sceptical little voice warned her, and when the first heavy drop of rain splashed on to the windscreen, Laura thrust her doubts aside and swung the car into the traffic to return to Bellavista.

It was at a party after the official opening of a new business complex in the city that Laura finally met Camilla von Dissel. She materialised among the hordes of people in a glittering black dress which was slit daringly from her shapely ankles to her thighs, and her hair, black as a raven's wing, was piled high on to her regally held head, the soft curls fastened with a large diamond clip which Laura swiftly calculated must have cost a small fortune.

'Darling!' she exclaimed in a low, musical voice as she swept across the floor towards them, and several heads turned just in time to witness Camilla embracing Anton and kissing him, European style, on both cheeks. Laura felt indignation drumming at her temples, but Camilla had not yet completed her act of possession. She stood close to Anton, her hands on his shoulders, and diamonds glittering at her smooth throat when she smiled up at him seductively. 'I've been hunting for you everywhere, and I was beginning to feel totally miserable thinking you hadn't come.'

Calm and seemingly unperturbed, Anton removed her hands from his shoulders, and kissed each one in turn while he smiled down at her with a warmth and affection that sent more than just a stab of envy through Laura's heart. She felt like an intruder standing there beside him, and then, as if suddenly remembering her presence, he made the necessary introductions.

Dark eyes, cold and assessing, met Laura's as they acknowledged each other, and instant dislike flared between them. Laura somehow managed to conceal her feelings, but Camilla made no effort to hide the fact that she considered Laura an insignificant nuisance and, turning towards Anton in a manner which excluded Laura completely, she linked her arm through his.

'Darling, I simply must see you alone,' she purred up at him persuasively. 'There's something terribly important I want to discuss with you, and we can't talk privately among all these people.'

Anton excused himself from Laura without hesitation and, leaving her standing there among an ocean of strange faces, he accompanied Camilla through the swinging glass doors, and out of sight.

'There goes a lady who drinks the milk of a viper each morning for breakfast,' a voice remarked knowingly behind her, and Laura swung round sharply to find herself staring up into the thin, intelligent face of a tall, lanky man with a familiar flashing smile. 'Alex Muir, remember?' he prodded her memory.

'Oh, yes,' she smiled, her brow clearing. 'We met at Gordon's Bay last month.'

'Madam, I'm flattered you should remember me,' he smiled, bowing towards her comically.

Relieved to see a familiar face, but curious, Laura asked, 'What are you doing here this evening? I mean,' she corrected herself blushingly, 'I never expected to see you here.'

He gestured vaguely with a slim-fingered, artistic hand. 'I did the décor.'

'I thought you said you were an artist,' she frowned up at him.

'My paintings don't bring in enough money,' he explained indulgently. 'And I have to eat.'

An awkward silence followed, and Laura's glance strayed involuntarily towards the glass doors through which Anton and Camilla had disappeared. Where were they? What were they doing?

'You look as though you could do with something to drink,' Alex interrupted her troubled thoughts, and, drawing her towards the drinks table, he asked, 'What will it be?'

'Something not too intoxicating,' she replied absently, wishing she could rid herself of that gnawing fear within her.

'I'll mix you one of my specials,' Alex offered, and seconds later a tall glass was placed in her hand.

'What is it?' she asked after a tentative sip at the amber-coloured liquid.

'Do you like it?'

She took another sip, and nodded appreciatively. 'It's nice, thank you.'

'Then don't ask questions, just drink it,' he ordered, taking her arm and leading her to a quiet corner behind the potted ferns. 'The Countess, I believe, is a very rich woman,' he said unexpectedly, staring down at the drink he swivelled in the glass between his fingers. 'Is your husband thinking of incorporating her wealth into his company?'

'I have no idea.'

'I hear they're old friends from way back when.'

Laura stiffened automatically. 'So I believe.'

Alex looked up from his drink, and smiled. 'You think I'm prying, don't you?'

'Aren't you?' she demanded with a haughtiness she had been forced to adopt at times.

'I'm curious,' he admitted without apology, his hazel eyes alert and probing. 'Why did you make no effort to stop her from dragging your husband off somewhere where she could have him to herself?'

Taut with resentment, she said stiffly, 'I think my husband is quite capable of looking after himself.'

'It's not your husband I'm concerned with.'

The words were quietly spoken, but their meaning was clear, and her resentment made way for a warmth which temporarily melted the icy feeling about her heart. 'Let's change the subject.'

'Right,' he smiled, swallowing down a mouthful of his drink before asking, 'Have you changed your mind yet about sitting for me?'

'No, I haven't.'

'Won't you give it a little serious thought?'

'Mr Muir——'

'Alex,' he corrected hastily.

'Alex,' she repeated resignedly. 'Why should you want to do a portrait of me?'

'Why *not*?' he laughed shortly.

'But it's absurd,' she argued. 'I'm not even beautiful.'

'You're a very attractive woman,' he contradicted, standing back a little to observe her critically. 'You have good bone structure, and a good figure, but your real beauty lies within. It's in your eyes, in the way you talk, and in the way you move. Very few women walk well,' he grimaced slightly. 'The Countess, for instance, sways her posterior too much, and although it's enchantingly seductive, it's not in the least graceful.'

'Oh, Alex,' she laughed, her misery momentarily forgotten. 'You're just saying this to make me feel better.'

'No, no, it's the truth,' he insisted adamantly above the noise as he dispensed with their glasses and gripped her hands tightly in his. 'I *must* paint you. I must capture what I see on canvas. It will be one of my masterpieces— I *know* it.'

She stared up at him thoughtfully, at the untidy sun-bleached hair which distinguished him from the rest despite his impeccably tailored evening suit, and at the enthusiasm glowing in his hazel eyes.

'You're really serious about this?' she asked at last.

'I'm more than serious,' he assured her with intense honesty. 'Now that I've seen you again, I'm *desperate*. Will you sit for me? Please?'

Beyond him she glimpsed Anton returning to the party alone and, disengaging her hands selfconsciously, she said: 'I'll let you know.'

'My number is in the book,' Alex reminded her, and she nodded briefly before making her way to Anton's side.

'I'm taking you home,' Anton announced brusquely, and without offering an explanation, he took her arm and led her from the building to where he had parked the Jaguar.

Bewildered, Laura remained silent during the long drive out to Bellavista. It was late, admittedly, but that was no reason why he should have said so bluntly, 'I'm taking you home.' Not *we*'re going home, but *you*. I'm taking *you* home. Had she done something wrong? she wondered frantically. Stepped on important toes, perhaps?

When the Jaguar crunched to a halt in front of the house, Laura was weary with the effort of trying to understand. They climbed the wide, shallow steps in silence up to the front door, the skirt of her evening gown swishing softly about her legs, and, stealing a quick glance at the man beside her who was her husband, yet at times like this a stranger, she felt the nerves tightening into a familiar knot at the pit of her stomach.

Anton unlocked the door and stood aside for her to enter, but when he did not follow her, she turned and asked nervously, 'Aren't you coming in as well?'

His mouth tightened as if her question had displeased him. 'I have urgent business to attend to. Lock the door and don't wait up for me.'

Dismayed, she stared after him, and only when the Jaguar's tail lights disappeared down the drive did she lock the door and go upstairs.

What urgent business would require his attention at this late hour? she wondered suddenly, dropping her wrap and evening purse on to the chair beside the window and pulling down the zip of her dress. Was it business? she wondered with sudden scepticism, or did Camilla's waiting arms have something to do with the urgency of this late-night mission?

'That's right! Torture yourself with your suspicious thoughts,' the voice of her conscience reprimanded her as she stepped out of her evening dress and hung it up in the wardrobe, but disturbing visions entered her mind, making a mockery of her determination to think no ill; visions of Anton and Camilla locked in each other's arms, their bodies close in a passionate embrace, and suddenly the room swayed about her, inducing a wave of nausea that sent her staggering through to the bathroom. She tried to control the spasms that wrenched her stomach, but couldn't, and for the first time since her childhood, she was violently sick.

Weak and exhausted, she finally emerged from the bathroom with barely enough energy left to get into bed and, with the immediate circumstances forcing her problems into the background, she promptly went to sleep.

She experienced a second flicker of nausea at the breakfast table the following morning, causing her to shun her usual bacon and eggs, and settling instead for a cup of black coffee. Fortunately Anton was too busy shutting himself away behind the morning newspaper to notice her physical discomfiture, and Sally was hurrying through her own breakfast before leaving for school. She must have eaten something at the party which had not agreed with her, Laura decided, and this led to further disturbing thoughts. What time had Anton finally returned home last night? What had been the true nature of the urgent business he had mentioned?

Anton slapped the folded newspaper down on to the table with a force that made her glance up at him with a guilty start, almost as if she suspected that he might have read her thoughts.

'I'll be home late tonight, so don't wait dinner for me,' he told her curtly, pushing back his chair and rising to his feet, then, with a brief nod, he was striding from the room.

'What's wrong with Uncle Anton?' Sally asked when they heard the Jaguar roar down the drive.

'Nothing—why?' Laura prevaricated, her nerves settling slowly into their correct order.

'He's different,' Sally announced frowningly. 'He's nearly always too busy to come home for dinner these days, and we hardly see him at weekends.'

'I think a man in his position must have tremendous problems to cope with,' Laura replied carefully.

'Well, I hope he solves his problems soon,' Sally said a little angrily, getting up from the table to kiss Laura's cheek. 'See you this afternoon.'

Laura watched her go and, sighing, she drew the newspaper towards her, curious to know what Anton had found so interesting, but there was nothing there except an announcement that, after a legal and financial tussle resulting from the untimely death of the Chairman of Avron Enterprises, the directors of the company had decided to sell to the highest bidder.

This did not affect Anton, surely? Not unless he intended placing a bid, of course, and if his bid was successful it would naturally result in added responsibilities. Did she have cause for concern, or was she merely leaping ahead into something which might never arise, and which Anton would rightly consider none of her business? From a medical point of view, Graham Abbot had long since given his valued opinion that Anton was heading towards a physical disaster, and suddenly Laura felt sick with anxiety. Nothing could be done, of course, until it was known for certain what Anton was planning, and the only one to discover this, without stirring up Anton's wrath, would be Graham Abbot.

Laura suddenly had an idea and, with Anton's eventual approval, she arranged a small, intimate dinner party for the Thursday evening to which she invited Graham and Gina Abbot. Graham, naturally, understood Laura's predicament, and agreed readily to do his best to discover Anton's intentions with regard to Avron Enterprises, and to dissuade him if necessary.

The evening was also intended to recapture some of their happier moments together before Camilla arrived on the scene, and Laura planned it with care, making certain that the menu consisted mainly of Anton's favourite dishes. Jemima too became fired with enthusiasm, as if she sensed the need for the evening to be a success, and when Sally complained about not being allowed to join the dinner party, it was Jemima who told her firmly, 'You will eat in the kitchen, Miss Sally, and no nonsense!'

Everything went smoothly until Anton arrived home that evening and altered the course of her plans, heading them towards an inevitable disaster.

'I've invited Camilla to join us for dinner this evening,' he announced as he passed Laura in the hall on his way upstairs to shower and change. 'One extra wouldn't upset your arrangements too much, would it?'

'Yes, yes, it *would* upset my arrangements!' she felt like shouting at him, but instead she stood there helplessly, feeling as though her world had suddenly collapsed beneath her as she said stonily, 'No, of course it wouldn't.'

What else could she say without making him suspect how vitally important this evening had been to her? She had never dreamed that something like this could happen, and never, *never* would she have thought that Anton would invite that abominable woman to his home. Was he actually such a fool as not to know that, having hurt him once, she could hurt him again?

Laura closed her eyes and prayed silently for strength. He had invited Camilla to dine with them, a woman he had once loved, and probably still loved if he stopped long enough to take stock of his feelings, and somehow Laura would have to bear it.

'That woman has come back here to make trouble, Miss Laura,' Jemima prophesied when Laura went through to the kitchen to inform her that there would be an extra guest. 'You mark my words, she's here to make trouble. It's in the stars.'

'Don't say that, Jemima,' Laura reprimanded her anxiously.

'I'm never wrong, Miss Laura,' Jemima insisted. 'When I saw you that very first time when you came here to Bellavista with young Miss Sally's mother and father, God rest their souls, I told Eddie you would one day be the mistress of Bellavista, and I was right. Now I'm telling you —with respect, madam—that woman is here to make trouble. *Big* trouble!'

Laura shivered as if a cold draught of wind had blown up against her. 'I hope you're wrong, Jemima.'

'Stand firm, Miss Laura,' the woman advised strongly. 'Don't let that woman drive away the happiness that belongs to Mr Anton and Bellavista.'

'What do you mean?'

Jemima must have thought her singularly dense, for she shook her head and smiled knowingly. 'When the fruit hangs heavy on the vines, you will be heavy with child.'

Heavy with child. Those words returned to Laura repeatedly, and, although she argued away the possibility, she could not deny that she had already begun to suspect that a new life had started its growth within her. It was an incredibly wonderful possibility, she realised, but a car was coming up the drive just as Anton entered the living-room, and she was forced to shelve her thoughts.

A strained silence hovered between Laura and Anton until a few minutes later when a waft of cold air entered the house with Camilla like the chilled hand of fate wrapping itself about Laura's heart, and she just barely managed to conceal the fact that she was shivering when the woman was shown into the living-room. Camilla was dressed in black once again, but this time in something a little less daring, and whether or not she happened to be in mourning, Laura had to admit that the colour suited this woman's olive-skinned complexion to perfection.

'I shall have to buy myself a car. Taxis are so unreliable,' she complained, extending her hands towards Anton and smiling up at him with an intimacy that lodged like a brick in Laura's throat. 'Darling, it's absolutely wonderful to be here at Bellavista again,' she purred. 'It's been such a long time, hasn't it?'

'More than eight years, if I remember correctly,' Anton smiled, raising her hands to his lips while Laura stood less than a yard away, ignored and feeling superfluous.

'We did have some wonderful times together, didn't we?' Camilla continued to weave her little cocoon of intimacy.

'Memorable times,' Anton agreed, releasing her hands and turning towards the cabinet where the drinks were kept. 'The usual, Camilla?'

'Thank you, darling,' she smiled, white teeth flashing against full, crimson lips as she draped her fur stole over the back of a chair.

'Good evening, Countess von Dissel.' Laura spoke for the first time, determined to make her presence known, and

Camilla turned, the smile still evident on her lips, but the dark eyes were calculatingly hard.

'Ah, the little wife. I never noticed you standing there.' Her disdainful glance swept up and down the length of Laura's taut, slender figure. 'You really shouldn't wear white, my dear, it makes you look awfully pale.'

It was a stab Laura should not have ignored, but Anton was pressing a glass of wine unceremoniously into her hand while extending a more lethal-looking drink towards Camilla.

'I hope it's to your taste?' he remarked, and Laura watched with infuriating helplessness while Camilla deliberately allowed her fingers to caress his hand before she took the glass from him.

'You're an angel,' she told him with that intimate, faintly seductive smile which Laura was beginning to hate with an intensity that threatened to choke her.

She clung to her control and remained silent, but she was fuming inwardly with a fury which stemmed from helpless despair as she observed them, and listened, like an unwanted third, to the undisguised intimacy in the trend of their conversation. What hope had she against a woman as beautiful as Camilla von Dissel, and what hope had Anton against the alluring charm of a woman who reminded Laura of a deadly black spider spinning her web with care in preparation for the kill?

Anton was not a fool, but he was, after all, only a man, and men were often trapped solely by desire.

CHAPTER EIGHT

THE chiming of the doorbell some minutes later came almost as a relief, and Laura excused herself, going into the hall seconds after Eddie had admitted Graham and Gina Abbot.

'My dear, you look lovely!' Gina exclaimed after Laura had welcomed them with a warmth which stemmed from affection and a liberal amount of desperation. 'Doesn't she look lovely, Graham?' Gina added, nudging her husband.

'Yes, yes,' the tall, grey-haired man nodded, his shrewd glance shifting from Laura's shadowed eyes to take in her slender figure. 'Laura always looks lovely to me, no matter what she's wearing.'

'Thank you,' Laura laughed self-consciously. 'You've both done a great deal to restore my confidence.'

From the inflection in her voice they must have guessed that something was amiss, but an explanation was unnecessary when they encountered Camilla in the living-room.

Anton was naturally pleased to see Graham and Gina, but the conversation flowed like sticky toffee flavoured with bitter aloe. Laura did her best to smooth over the uneven patches, while Camilla, with clever subtlety, somehow managed to point out and criticise every alteration Laura had made to add a little of her own personality to Bella-vista's living-room. Anton, obviously, found it amusing, but Graham puffed away furiously as his cigar, which was a sure sign that he felt uncomfortable and agitated.

Laura could no longer ignore the frantic little signs Gina was making in her direction when she thought no one was looking, and she finally excused herself with, 'I must see if Sally's all right.'

'I'm coming with you,' Gina said at once. 'I haven't seen the child in ages.'

They crossed the hall and climbed the stairs, but the moment they were out of earshot, Gina remarked caustically, 'I didn't know Camilla would be here this evening.'

'Neither did I until Anton arrived home and sprang it on me,' Laura confessed with a hint of bitterness in her voice.

'Heavens, the woman is a pain in the neck!' Gina hissed angrily. 'What on earth does Anton think he's doing, encouraging her in this way?'

'I don't know what Anton has in mind, but I'm beginning to see what *she's* aiming at.'

'So can I,' Gina remarked in a tight-lipped fashion. 'She's doing her level best to make you feel cheap and inferior, and Anton just sits there calmly and lets her get away with it.' An exclamation of disgust passed her lips. 'Really, the man must be insane!'

'Oh, Gina, what am I going to do?' Laura asked when they paused on the landing which led off to Sally's room.

'Fight back, my dear.'

'How? And with what?' Laura asked desperately.

Gina gestured angrily. 'For goodness' sake, Laura, you're his *wife*!'

'His wife on sufferance, yes,' Laura said softly, a faintly cynical smile twisting her lips as she absently fingered the necklace at her throat which Anton had given her on her birthday.

'You're still his wife, and that gives you a considerable advantage over her,' Gina insisted, gripping Laura's arms and shaking her slightly. 'You can't just sit back and do nothing while that witch claws her way back into his life.'

With Gina's words ringing in Laura's ears, they went to Sally's room and found her poring over a new adventure novel which Laura had bought for her.

'Who's that lady who came in the taxi?' she wanted to

know eventually, and when they told her, she pulled a face and said: 'I don't like her.'

'Neither do we,' Laura and Gina chorussed without hesitation, then, glancing at each other, they laughed a little crazily.

'We'd better not leave Graham alone with them much longer,' Laura said at length, and they left a puzzled-looking Sally behind to return to the living-room.

Camilla's personality was overpowering. She dominated the conversation at the dinner table much the same as a bullfighter dominated the attention of the bloodthirsty spectators, but Graham was a patient man, and when the opportunity arose, he leapt into the arena.

'I believe Avron Enterprises are selling out to the highest bidder.'

Graham's remark seemed to cloy the air like an ignited fuse, and Laura waited with bated breath for some sort of explosion when she glanced at Anton's hard, expressionless face, but he merely nodded briefly and said in his usual abrupt manner, 'That's right.'

'I've heard a rumour that you might be interested,' Graham ventured a shot in the dark with a casualness Laura was beginning to admire.

'I am,' Anton stunned them with his reply. 'I've entered into negotiations on Camilla's behalf.'

Never in a thousand years could Laura have explained her feelings at that moment as she stared down the length of the table at the man who faced her with a cynical smile playing about his mouth.

'*You* want to buy Avron Enterprises?' Graham demanded of Camilla when he had overcome his astonishment.

'Yes, I do,' she smiled, a gleam of satisfaction in those hard eyes. 'Does that surprise you, Graham?'

'Do you intend to compete against Anton's firm?' Gina questioned her directly when Graham seemed at a loss for words.

'Oh, goodness, no! I'm sure Anton and I could work in close harmony together without becoming nasty competitors.' Camilla placed a possessive, bejewelled hand on Anton's arm and smiled at him in her most seductive manner. 'Couldn't we, darling?'

Anton placed his hand over hers and smiled back at her with an undisguised intimacy that stabbed viciously at Laura's heart. 'I see no reason why our two firms couldn't combine in a united effort.'

'Depending, of course, on whether Camilla's bid is successful or not,' Gina cut in, flashing Laura a glance which said: 'If *you* don't claw the bitch's eyes out, then *I'll* do it for you!'

Anton released Camilla's hand and placed his table napkin beside his plate as he said calmly, 'Avron Enterprises won't receive a better offer than the one Camilla has made.'

'So it's all settled, then?' Gina asked, her mouth set in a thin line of disapproval.

'Not quite,' Anton smiled indulgently. 'These things take time.'

'And I have all the time in the world, darling,' Camilla added, a suggestive intonation in her low, musical voice which was unmistakable.

Laura could suddenly take no more and, getting to her feet abruptly, she said: 'Shall we have coffee in the living-room?'

'Good idea,' Graham agreed, a look of displeasure on his lean face as he followed her example and pushed back his chair.

The others followed suit, and the agonising evening progressed, punctuated with strained silences, until Graham and Gina announced that it was time they went home. Anton accompanied Laura to the door to see them off, and she was intensely relieved when Camilla draped her fur stole about her shoulders a few minutes later and prepared to leave.

'We'll see each other again, I'm sure, and do thank Jemima for me,' she said, turning to Laura in the hall and delivering her parting shot. 'How fortunate for you to have Jemima to depend on. She knows Bellavista like the back of her hand, and when it comes to the organisation of a home this size, not to mention the planning of the dinners, you would do well to take a few hints from her, because this evening's dinner was superb.'

Laura considered this a deliberate insult when she took into consideration the hours she had spent planning the menu for which Jemima was now receiving the praise. It was also a blatant insinuation that she lacked the intelligence to cope, and Laura's anger flared like a red-hot fire in her breast.

'My car's waiting, Camilla,' Anton forestalled Laura just as she was about to explode, and Camilla turned towards him with a triumphant smile to lay a caressing hand against his cheek.

'Darling, you're an absolute angel to drive me home,' she purred and, nodding briefly in Laura's direction, she swept out of the house.

'I'll be back as soon as I can,' said Anton, and then the door closed behind him, leaving Laura alone in the hall.

She stared at the heavy oak door through a red mist of fury, and it was some time before she managed to control herself sufficiently to put out the lights and climb the stairs up to the bedroom Anton seldom shared with her now. The intimate dinner party, which she had arranged with such care, had turned into a fiasco, and it had also been a painful demonstration of how little consideration she could expect from Anton. Added to this, he had behaved abominably towards Graham and Gina. He had given most of his attention to Camilla, and Laura felt that she could not blame their friends if they never set foot on Bellavista's soil again.

Laura went to bed, but she could not sleep, and she lay there staring up at the white ceiling with its heavy wooden

beams, her feelings fluctuating from anger to despair.
Anton had been away almost two hours; long enough for
him to have driven Camilla home and returned to Bellavista twice. What were they *doing*? Were they discussing
business, or were they reliving passionate memories in
each other's arms?

'Oh, God, please help me! Please, *please* help me!' she
groaned, switching off the light and burying her face in the
pillow in an effort to shut out the pain.

Moments later the sound of a car approaching the house
made her sit up in bed with a jerk. She recognised the
sound of the Jaguar's engine, and lay back against the
pillows, her body tense as she listened, and waited. Several
minutes passed before she heard Anton's heavy, muted
footsteps coming down the carpeted passage, and suddenly
she knew she could not bear to see him. She turned over
on to her side and closed her eyes, pretending to be asleep,
but her nerves vibrated like a tightly coiled spring when she
heard the door being opened and closed. Seconds later the
light was switched on beside her, and the bed sagged
beneath his hands as he stood leaning over her.

'Don't pretend you're asleep, Laura, because I know
you're not,' he accused mockingly, and her eyes flew open
at once to find him bending low over her.

'Don't touch me!' she cried out in disgust, shrinking
from him mentally and physically as her nostrils were
filled with Camilla's heavy, exotic scent. 'You're reeking
of that woman's perfume,' she accused sharply.

'Hm ...' He sniffed himself appreciatively, and smiled as
if he were recalling something pleasant. 'A very exciting
perfume. You should ask her for the name, and use it
yourself.'

'It would make me sick!'

'Pity,' he shrugged nonchalantly as he moved away from
her and took off his jacket and tie. He flung them on to a
chair and calmly proceeded to unbutton his shirt.

'Why did you invite her here this evening?' Laura demanded, observing the gradual exposure of his broad, hair-roughened chest with a hypnotic fascination.

'She's an old friend, and I happen to like her company.'

'Well, I *don't*!' she almost shouted at him. 'She was stifling, to say the least.'

Anton's shirt joined his jacket and tie on the chair, then he calmly unbuckled his belt, his eyes mocking her ruthlessly as he said accusingly, 'You're jealous.'

Laura sat bolt upright in bed. '*Jealous?*' she shrieked with angry indignation. 'Of *her*? You must be mad!'

'She has a damn sight more poise and charm than you're displaying at the moment,' Anton continued calmly and infuriatingly as he dropped his belt on the floor and seated himself at the foot of the bed to remove his shoes and socks.

'Poised she may be, but her charm left much to be desired,' argued Laura, caught up in a passionate fury she had never experienced before. '*Dahling,*' she mimicked Camilla's voice to perfection. 'Do you remember that fabulously exciting weekend we spent at that little hotel in the mountains? You were such an absolute angel, *dahling.*'

'You little vixen,' he laughed, reaching for her, but she shrank from him with an exclamation of disgust.

'Don't you dare touch me!' she spat at him. 'I won't have you coming to me directly from that woman's arms.'

'We shall see about that,' he snapped, ruthless hands dragging her back against the pillows when she tried to escape, and then he was pinning her down with the weight of his body.

'Have you no sense of decency?' she cried, fighting him off like a wildcat with every particle of strength she possessed, but he stripped her effortlessly until nothing stood in the way of his questing hands. 'I hate you!' she screamed at him, her eyes filling with tears. 'I hate you, do you hear?'

'Shut up!' he ordered harshly, his lips like fire against her throat.

'I won't shut up! I hate you, I——'

His mouth silenced hers with effective brutality, but this did not deter her from fighting him every step of the way until, shamed at the way her flesh responded to his touch, she called him every kind of hateful name under the sun. Somehow, she had no idea when, he had divested himself of the rest of his clothes, and when she felt that hard, muscular body against her own, she began to realise the futility of her efforts. Anton's expertise as a lover wore down her resistance until an intolerable surge of excitement forced a cry of pleasure from her lips, and the hands which had clawed and pushed at his shoulders moments before now gripped tightly as desire drugged her mind and ruled her body.

Nothing mattered at that moment, not even the faint suggestion of Camilla's perfume which she felt certain still clung to him, and, grasping a handful of his crisp, dark hair, she drew his head down on to her breast and surrendered herself to the emotions only he could arouse in her.

Anton was dressed and ready to leave for the office when Laura awoke the following morning, and she observed him through lowered lashes when he crossed the room to open the curtains.

'There's a heavy mist on the mountain which is not unusual for this time of the year,' he remarked, turning towards her and trailing his glance over her shape beneath the sheet as if calling to mind every part of her body. 'I'll be home late this evening. I'm dining out with Camilla.'

The mention of Camilla's name, after what had happened the previous evening, was like waving a red flag at a bull, and Laura sat up in bed with a start. 'You're the most disgusting, the most despicable—oh, I *hate* you!'

She flung a pillow at him, wishing it was something lethal, but Anton caught it smartly and flung it back at her with a force that knocked her back against the pillows.

'It seems as though I married a little spitfire,' he mocked her as he approached the bed, and his mockery added fuel to the fire of her anger.

'How dare you treat me like this! Flaunting your affair with that woman in my face is positively indecent!'

'I'm not answerable to you for anything I might do,' he said gratingly as he leaned over her, and his attitude was all at once so menacing that she clutched the pillow against her breast like a shield.

'I don't deserve to be treated like this, Anton. I'm your wife.'

His mouth hardened into a thin, ominous line. 'A wife is nothing but a glorified mistress, and that's all I require from you, so don't imagine it gives you the right to dictate my actions to me.'

Laura flinched when he slammed the bedroom door behind him moments later, but she lay there dry-eyed and with a sick feeling at the pit of her stomach as she stared up at the ceiling. *A wife is nothing but a glorified mistress,* he had said. *A glorified mistress!* The words reverberated through her mind and seared through her soul like a red-hot poker. She threw aside the pillow and sat up, but a wave of nausea sent her rushing through to the bathroom, and later, when she leaned weakly against the basin, she stared at her white face in the mirror, and knew the worst. She was going to have his child!

She went down to breakfast an hour later and caught Sally on her way out. Sally took one look at Laura and exclaimed, 'You look terrible!'

Laura had always found her childish candour amusing, but at that moment she felt very much like bursting into tears as she dropped a light kiss on the little girl's forehead and pushed her towards the door. 'You'll be late for school.'

On the steps Sally paused and glanced back at her with concern. 'I hope you feel better this afternoon.'

With Sally's departure a silence settled about the house which Laura found utterly depressing. The silence had never troubled her before, but she would go mad with nothing to do until her niece returned home that afternoon, she thought frantically as she helped herself to a cup of coffee.

The shrill ringing of the telephone half an hour later jarred her fragile nerves, but it was almost a relief to be doing something, and she hurried into the hall to answer it.

'Laura DeVere?' a man's voice questioned abruptly.

'Yes,' she replied hesitantly, trying to place him.

'Alex Muir,' he announced, setting her mind at rest. 'Look, I know you told me you'd let me know what you've decided, but for days now I've been staring at that rough sketch I made of you, and I wondered . . .' There was an embarrassed silence, then he asked, 'What about it, Laura?'

'Alex, I . . . don't know, I . . .'

'Please?' he begged. 'I'm fired with inspiration at the moment, and you wouldn't want it all to go to waste, would you?'

Laura hesitated, but already the idea was beginning to appeal to her. It would be an excuse to get out of the house, and it would be something with which to fill the empty hours until Sally returned home in the afternoons.

'How long will it take?' she asked, not quite sure yet what to do.

'A week—maybe two.'

'Why not?' a little voice urged her, and before she could change her mind, she asked, 'When do you want me there?'

'Right now, if you can make it,' Alex replied, unable to hide the excitement in his voice, and Laura smiled faintly when she heard it.

'Give me your address,' she said without further consideration, and scribbled it down hastily before ringing off.

Alex's Sea Point flat had an excellent view of the sea, Laura discovered less than an hour later, and it looked more like a workshop than a place to live in. Paintings ranging from landscapes to portraits were propped up against the walls, and the place reeked of turpentine and oils.

'Lady, I shall always be grateful to you,' Alex smiled at her as he led her across the room towards the largest window. 'Would you like something to drink before we start?'

Laura shook her head nervously. 'No, thank you.'

'Right,' he nodded abruptly, looking extremely business-like now as he gestured towards a long, low stool. 'Sit there, if you don't mind. Draw your legs up under you a little, and look towards the window. You can see the ocean, can't you?'

'Yes,' she smiled nervously, doing as she was told.

'Now just relax. Be comfortable, and imagine you're sitting on the rocks at Gordon's Bay.' He observed her critically for a moment, then his lean features broke into a smile of approval. 'That's it!'

He picked up his easel and, placing it a little distance from her, began to work with quick, deft strokes.

'May I talk?' Laura asked at length when her thoughts began to dwell on the painful confrontation she had had with Anton that morning. 'Or do you need silence when you work?'

'You may talk as much as you like,' he assured her, his quick smile flashing at her across the easel.

'I couldn't help noticing all those framed paintings lean-ing against the walls,' she said. 'Are you planning an ex-hibition of some sort?'

'Yes, I am, and if this portrait turns out to be what I'm hoping for, then it will be the highlight of the exhibition.'

Laura digested this for a moment in silence before she laughed selfconsciously and said: 'I'm not sure whether I should feel flattered or nervous.'

Hazel eyes laughed at her across the easel. 'You have nothing to feel nervous about. That's my department en-tirely, so just relax.'

During the following two weeks Laura sat for Alex every morning, except weekends, and during those morning sessions she began to look upon him as a friend. He made her laugh a lot, which was something she had not done for a long time, but most of all those hours spent with him in his improvised studio made her forget temporarily that Anton was almost constantly in Camilla's company. She was intensely curious, however, to see the painting, but Alex was adamant. 'No one sees it until it's completed,' he had said, and she had left it at that.

'Loosen your hair,' he told her when she came for one of her last sittings. 'I want to concentrate on your features this morning.'

Laura did as she was told, and drew it forward across her shoulder as he instructed, 'Is this how you want it?'

'That's just fine,' he said, eyeing her critically before he set to work. 'How's the merry widow?'

'I beg your pardon?' she asked, glancing at him blankly.

'Look out of the window,' he ordered sharply, and when she had done so, he explained, 'I'm talking about the luscious Countess von Dissel. Have you seen her lately?'

Her eyes clouded. 'No.'

'She's a thorn in your side, isn't she?'

'Yes,' Laura admitted, bitterness welling up inside her.

'How does your husband feel about her?'

'He thinks her charming, and poised, and very beautiful, naturally,' she said tritely, driving the sword into her own heart with every painful word she uttered.

'Old love dies hard, they say,' Alex observed dryly.

'Yes.' The sword twisted, adding to her suffering.

'Did you marry him for your niece's sake?'

Startled, she asked, 'What on earth makes you think that?'

'People talk,' Alex said absently. 'You know how it is.'

A look of distaste crossed her face. 'You shouldn't lend out your ears to gossip, Alex.'

'I don't usually, but when it's about someone I admire and respect very much, then I can't help listening and wondering,' he explained calmly, almost casually. 'You're not happy, I know that, and if those rumours are true ...'

He left his sentence unfinished, and Laura stared thoughtfully at the ever-changing face of the sea for a time before she sighed audibly. 'I hardly know you, Alex, but for some reason I like you, and trust you.'

'What you're actually trying to tell me is that those rumours are true.'

It was a statement, not a question, and she nodded slightly. 'Yes, they're true.'

His shrewd glance observed her for a moment across the easel. 'Am I right in suspecting you've fallen in love with your husband?'

'You're very astute,' she smiled, but her smile was tinged with sadness.

'As an artist I have to be,' he stated calmly, and worked on in silence for several minutes before he asked, 'Does he know how you feel about him?'

'No.'

'Don't you think it would make a difference if he knew?'

'It would make matters worse, and besides ...' Laura paused, her eyes darkening with pain, 'what chance do I have against someone as beautiful as Camilla?'

'You must credit your husband with some sense, Laura,' Alex said in a faintly reprimanding voice. 'He's not an imbecile.'

'I never said he *was*, but——'

'Isn't he worth fighting for?' Alex interrupted.

'Oh, Alex ...' she laughed, but her laughter was laced with bitterness. 'I'm way out of my depth, and I know it. I always thought that loving someone came simply and naturally, but instead I find myself in a situation where I feel like a novice playing a game without knowing the rules. It's like being on a battlefield with everyone shouting "Fight, fight!" but there are no weapons about.'

'You have the strongest weapon in your possession,' Alex told her, and when she ventured a curious glance in his direction, he added: 'Love.'

'Love?' she repeated stupidly.

'Do you think the Countess is really capable of offering him a deep, abiding love which is as unselfish and undemanding as yours?' A disparaging sound passed his lips before he continued. 'She's a cold fish, Laura. Her love could be measured by a man's bank balance, and if that should ever dwindle, then so would her love—and very quickly too, I might add.'

Laura did not doubt the validity of that statement, but at that moment there was something more important to consider, and she grimaced as she said: 'I think I'm developing a cramp.'

'Take a break,' he said at once, putting down his brushes and palette. 'I'll make us a pot of tea.'

Laura stretched her legs and arched her back, then she walked across to the window and stared down into the street below. The traffic never ceased, and neither did the noise, but beyond it lay the ocean, calm and untroubled with the waves washing out on to the rocky beach in an almost leisurely fashion. If only her life could be as calm and untroubled as the sea that morning, she thought with a sigh. She had confided in Alex more than she had done with anyone else, and it had been a relief to talk about it, but she had still come no nearer to finding a solution. There was no magic wand that she could wave; no instant remedy for a heart that ached for a love it could never have, and she somehow had the feeling that time was running out on her.

Her session with Alex lasted longer than usual that day, and it was almost two o'clock when she finally stepped out of the building and into the wintery sunshine.

'Well, imagine meeting you here,' a familiar voice stopped Laura in her tracks, and she turned to see Camilla walking towards her. 'Have you been visiting a friend?' she asked, gesturing towards the building Laura had just left. 'Or were you hoping to discover where I lived?'

'I was visiting a friend,' Laura assured her hastily, feeling unaccountably nervous. 'If you'll excuse me, I——'

'Don't go yet.' A bejewelled hand gripped Laura's arm. 'There's a tea-room across the street, and it's time you and I had a little talk.'

'Really, Countess von Dissel, I can't think of anything you and I have in common that needs discussing.'

'It concerns Anton.'

'Anton?' Laura asked sharply, cold fear gripping her heart.

'I thought that would interest you.' Camilla smiled that humourless smile which Laura knew could only spell danger, and, releasing Laura's arm, suggested confidently, 'Shall we go?'

Laura nodded, but she knew that nothing good could come of this meeting with the beautiful Countess von Dissel, only heartache.

In the beachfront tea-room overlooking the swimming pools and rock gardens, Laura sat facing Camilla across the small table. Their tea had arrived, and Camilla had poured, but they had exchanged nothing but senseless platitudes which had only served to increase Laura's tension.

'Countess, I'm in rather a hurry, and Sally will be home soon,' Laura said eventually when she could stand it no longer. 'Shall we get to the point?'

'Very well, darling, we'll get straight to the point, as you say.' The smile of false geniality vanished, and Laura found herself staring into the cold, hard eyes of her enemy. 'I want Anton.'

Laura felt her insides lurch sickeningly, but except for a faint whiteness about her mouth, her expression remained miraculously cool and unperturbed as she said calmly, 'You should tell Anton that, not me.'

A semblance of a smile touched that hard but beautiful mouth. 'I already have, darling, but I think it's only fair that you should know about it.'

'And now that I do know, what do you expect me to do about it?'

'Leave him, or give him sufficient reason to divorce you.'

Laura drew a careful, agonising breath. 'You've discussed this with Anton?'

'Naturally.'

'And if I refuse to do as you both obviously want?'

'Darling, everyone knows you married each other for the child's sake,' Camilla laughed softly, but her laughter was venomous. 'You wouldn't want to force Anton to continue with this marriage when you know his interests are elsewhere, would you?'

'Anton is Sally's guardian, and he would never shirk his responsibilities.'

'Naturally,' Camilla smiled again, 'but carrying out his responsibilities doesn't necessarily mean that he must continue with a marriage which is beginning to bore him, does it?'

He was bored with their marriage, and bored with her! Those words, like carefully directed barbs, found their mark with painful precision.

'Has he asked you to marry him?' Laura asked at length when she was able to trust her voice.

'How can he while he's still married to you?'

'He's led you to believe, though, that he wants to marry you,' Laura persisted, driving the painful barbs deeper into her own heart.

'If I didn't believe it, then I wouldn't be sitting here talking to you like this, would I?' Camilla smiled coldly, a gleam of triumph in her dark eyes as she saw the colour drain from Laura's face.

She had won, and she knew it, Laura thought as helplessness and despair settled about her like a heavy cloak. 'You have the strongest weapon in your possession,' she recalled Alex's words. *Love!* It was like sitting with an ace up her sleeve, but with no opportunity to play it, she realised dismally.

'Why didn't you marry Anton years ago when you had

the opportunity?' she asked at last, staring down into her untouched cup of tea.

'Darling, I was young and foolish, and we'd argued. I took the argument seriously, and married Karl von Dissel on the rebound.' Camilla paused effectively, her features assuming a suitable expression of regret which lacked conviction to the discerning eye. 'It was a mistake,' she continued. 'I know that now, and I ruined the lives of three people—Karl's, Anton's, and my own.'

'And you're about to ruin mine,' the words sprang to mind, but they remained unuttered as Laura unclenched her hands in her lap and picked up her handbag. 'Was there anything else you wanted to tell me?' she asked coldly.

'No, my dear, except ...' Camilla's smile was chilling ... 'don't stand in the way of Anton's happiness. It would be spiteful and childish of you.'

Laura drove back to Bellavista that day in a numbed state of indecision and uncertainty. She had to think, but her brain refused to co-operate, and she spent the afternoon merely going through the motions of attending to Sally's needs.

'I'm going for a walk,' she said at last, hoping the fresh air would clear her mind and lift the veil of depression which had settled about her.

'But it's almost time for dinner,' Sally wailed in protest.

'I'll be back in time,' Laura murmured distractedly as she stepped out on to the sunstoep and, without thinking, chose the path leading towards the slope of the mountain.

She walked briskly at first, and then slower as the agonising memory of her conversation with Camilla washed over her. Her brain was suddenly alive; frantically alive as it darted from one aching thought to the next until she cried out in silent desperation.

'I *can't* let him marry Camilla. She'll hurt him again. She'll ruin him for ever. I *can't* let him go. I *won't*! I'm going to have his child, and when he knows ...'

She was climbing now. Higher and higher, unaware of where she was going, and unaware of the descending mist becoming denser by the second. She was fighting a lonely, desperate battle with herself, and she was losing. If what Camilla had said was the truth, then Anton should have his freedom.

'I can't keep him tied to me,' Laura spoke out loud into the mist without quite realising it, and her voice sounded raw and quite unlike her own. 'I can't hold him against his will; not for Sally's sake, and *never* for the sake of the child I'm carrying. I couldn't bear it if he stayed with me for that reason. I just *couldn't*!'

That was her last conscious thought before her feet slipped from under her. Her head struck something hard, there was a blinding flash of pain, and then she sank willingly into the dark pit of oblivion which seemed to open up in front of her.

CHAPTER NINE

LAURA had no idea how long she had lain there on the mountain, but she came to her senses with the realisation that she was cold and uncomfortably wet. It was dark, and her head throbbed painfully with every beat of her heart. Where was she? she wondered frantically, trying to sit up, but her head ached to such an extent that she groaned and lowered herself on to the uneven ground once more. She had no idea which way she had come, and Anton had warned her once of the hidden dangers when out climbing in the mist.

'Stay away from the mountain,' he had said, 'but if you're ever caught up there in the mist, don't panic, and stay where you are until help arrives.'

'Don't panic and stay where you are,' she repeated to herself. It was helpful advice, but, heaven help her, she was wet through and shivering with cold, and her head felt as if it wanted to burst. Somewhere, through the deathly silence of the mist, a voice was calling out a name at regular intervals, and she went colder still as she recalled the story of Friedrich walking the mist at night in search of Dora, the woman he had loved.

Was that someone calling her name? she wondered, straining her ears. Or was it Dora?

'That would depend on whether it was Friedrich or Anton out there roaming the mist,' she finally concluded a little hysterically.

She tried to cry out, but no sound passed her lips as she waited in a mixture of terror and hope for the owner of that voice to reach her. An eternity seemed to pass before her terrified eyes glimpsed a dark shape emerging from the mist, but then she wished that she had been less eager.

'Oh, God, it's Friedrich,' she thought hysterically as she turned her eyes away from the blinding light flashed at her, but there was nothing ghostly about the muttered oath that reached her ears, nor in the strong arms lifting her, and when her throbbing head came to rest on a familiar shoulder, she suddenly knew no more.

She rose eventually to a level of consciousness where she became aware of lying on a bed. Strong, yet surprisingly gentle, hands removed her wet clothes from her shivering body, and she was wrapped in something warm and dry. It was Anton. She knew his touch. But for once she did not mind, and as he pulled the blankets up about her, she sighed and slipped deeper into the vale of darkness from which she emerged again much later to find Graham Abbot bending over her anxiously.

'Well, you've certainly taken your time about waking up, haven't you?' he teased, his finger lingering on her pulse.

'What time is it?' she asked weakly, fully conscious now.

'Almost eleven o'clock.'

'Almost eleven?' Laura sat up with a jerk, only to fall back against the pillows a moment later when a stab of pain tore through her temples. 'Oh, my head!' she groaned.

'You have a nasty bump there, but all in all you've had a lucky escape,' Graham told her lightly.

'A lucky escape from what?' she grunted, examining the egg-shaped lump against the side of her head with gentle fingers.

'Pneumonia for one,' Graham replied dryly. 'You must have been lying unconscious for almost three hours before Anton found you.'

'When he came out of the mist towards me I thought for one terrible moment that it was Friedrich's ghost,' she confessed.

'You've been paying too much attention to Jemima's fanciful stories of old Friedrich's restless spirit roaming the mountain at night,' Graham laughed, his grey eyes dancing, then he shot a question at her that plunged her back into reality with sickening speed. 'Did you know you're pregnant?'

'I suspected it,' she whispered, then a terrible thought came to mind, and she glanced anxiously at the lean, grey-haired man while he closed his medical bag and pocketed his stethoscope. 'Graham, you haven't told Anton, have you?'

'No,' he laughed, seating himself on the bed. 'Women usually prefer telling their husbands in their own good time.'

'He must never know, Graham.'

'But, my dear girl——'

'I mean it,' she interrupted urgently.

'But *why*, for heaven's sake?' Graham demanded incredulously, observing her with a clinical eye as if he suspected that she might have become deranged.

'I had quite an interesting discussion with Camilla this afternoon. It seems——' Laura felt choked suddenly, but she had to go on. 'It seems as though it won't be long before Anton asks for his freedom.'

'What nonsense!'

'Oh, Graham,' she sighed, suddenly feeling incredibly tired, 'you read the newspapers just as I do, and you know what they're saying about Anton and Camilla.'

He gestured angrily. 'It's all pure conjecture.'

'Is it?' Her soft mouth quivered and twisted bitterly. 'Are the photographs that were taken of them together over the past two weeks also a projected image of some reporter's imagination?'

'It could have something to do with Camilla buying Avron Enterprises,' he suggested. 'Have you thought of that?'

She nodded, but a sharp pain made her wince and grab her head. 'I've thought of that,' she groaned, 'but I don't think I can believe that any more.'

'Laura ...' Graham shook his head a little helplessly, 'I

don't know what to say to you.'

She clutched anxiously at the hand nearest to her. 'All I want is your word that you won't tell Anton about— about the baby.'

'If that's what you want, yes,' he nodded thoughtfully. 'Would you like me to talk to him about this business with Camilla?'

'I'll talk to him myself. I think I——'

The sound of the bedroom door opening made her break off in mid-sentence, and Anton's voice asked in an oddly hushed way, 'How is she?'

'Ask her yourself,' said Graham, getting to his feet and placing a small phial of capsules on the bedside table. 'Don't get up tomorrow unless you feel up to it,' he told Laura. 'And take one of these capsules every three hours for the pain, if necessary.'

'Thank you, Graham,' she smiled up at him. 'I'm sorry my foolishness kept you out so late.'

'All in a day's work,' he assured her, squeezing her shoulder lightly. 'I'll see myself out,' he said to Anton as he passed him on his way to the door.

Laura's heart was beating heavily against her ribs when she found herself alone with Anton a few seconds later. He approached the bed slowly and sat down beside her, but she avoided the probing intensity of his glance.

'How do you feel?' he asked at last, breaking the peculiar silence between them.

'My head aches, but otherwise I'm fine.' Those heavy-lidded eyes glittered strangely as they travelled over her, seeking their own reassurance, and her hands fluttered nervously as she straightened the sheets about her, almost as if she were afraid he would guess her secret. 'I'm sorry to have caused you so much trouble,' she apologised unsteadily.

'My God, what were you trying to do?' he exploded unexpectedly with a violence that made her jump. 'Kill yourself?' he added harshly.

'What happened wasn't intentional, and I've said I'm sorry,' she reminded him agitatedly.

He stared hard at her for long, tense seconds, the line of his jaw taut, then he got to his feet and walked some distance away from her as if he could not bear to be near her. 'I'll get you something to eat,' he said, turning towards the door.

'Please, I—I couldn't eat anything now.'

He nodded slowly. 'I'd better leave you, then, to get some rest.'

'Before you go, Anton, there's something I—I have to say to you.'

'You're tired, Laura,' he said roughly, his hand resting on the polished brass handle of the door. 'Won't it keep until morning?'

'No, it won't,' she insisted, and her mouth went dry as he moved away from the door to stand just beyond the circle of light coming from the bedside lamp. She passed the tip of her tongue nervously across her lips, and swallowed. 'Please, Anton, I—I want you to know that I—I'll give you your freedom whenever you want it.'

A deathly silence settled in the room, and, just for one fleeting moment, she wondered if it had not been a mistake to let him know that she was aware of his desire to end their marriage, but the next moment he set her mind, if not her heart, at rest by saying coldly, 'That's very generous of you, Laura. I shall keep that in mind.'

Laura felt peculiarly drained of emotion when the door closed behind him seconds later, and not even when she heard the Jaguar being driven at speed from the house did she feel anything other than the dull pain in her injured head. Anton was going to Camilla, of course, and he was understandably in a hurry to tell her that his wife had announced herself willing to free him. How thrilled Camilla would be at the news of her easy victory—how triumphant! But what did it matter? Laura thought dully. Nothing mattered now any more—nothing at all!

Sally and Jemima greeted Laura with concern when she came down to breakfast the following morning, but fortunately she was able to assure them that, apart from a slight headache, she ailed nothing more. She told Gina the same when she telephoned minutes after Sally had been driven off to school, and an hour later Laura was driving herself to Sea Point for her usual session with Alex.

Laura was coming down Bellavista's wide staircase late the following afternoon when she heard raised voices in the hall below, and she hurried down the rest of the way to find Eddie involved in a verbal altercation with a young man who looked vaguely familiar. She stepped warily into the hall and asked, 'What's the problem, Eddie?'

'This gentleman is from the newspapers, madam, and Mr Anton said——'

'We've met before, Mrs DeVere. On the day after your sister and brother-in-law died, to be exact,' the young man interrupted, and when her brow cleared on recognition, he added cheekily, 'On that occasion I was ordered off the property, but this time I have information you would be well advised to listen to.'

'Shall I see him off the premises, madam?' Eddie asked, his manner threatening.

'No, Eddie,' Laura said at once. 'I'll see Mr ...'

'Farrell,' the young man supplied his name. 'Tim Farrell.'

'Come this way, Mr Farrell,' Laura gestured towards the living-room, and the reporter smiled triumphantly at the glowering Eddie as he stepped into the hall and followed Laura. 'You said you had information. What information are you referring to?' she questioned once they were seated.

'Robert Dean had been on a friendly mission for one of our oil companies to an oil-producing state in North Africa. He stopped over at Walvis Bay, and on that same night a Russian trawler made an unscheduled stop at that same harbour,' Tim Farrell explained without hesitation. 'One of the crew was taken off the trawler with suspected appendicitis, but it was a false alarm, and the trawler left again before dawn.'

Laura hid her surprise admirably behind her controlled features. 'What are you trying to say, Mr Farrell?'

'The trawler had docked next to the *Bluebird*, and, according to my informant, your sister and brother-in-law spent the evening with friends, leaving the *Bluebird* unguarded.'

'I still don't understand what you're getting at.'

Tim Farrell smiled that cheeky, triumphant smile as he delivered the conclusion to his story. 'If my theories are correct, then the trawler's unscheduled stop was planned and, as fate would have it, they had an ideal opportunity to plant that bomb on board the yacht.'

'You're merely supposing, Mr Farrell,' she said with a coldness that matched the chill in her veins.

'Not everything I've told you is supposition, Mrs DeVere, and unless you can prove me wrong, this story is going into print tomorrow.'

Was this some form of moral blackmail? Laura wondered, suppressing her anger and her fears with difficulty as she said: 'I'm afraid I can't confirm or deny your theories, but I——'

'Then my story goes into print as it is,' he announced flatly, preparing to leave.

'Mr Farrell, I must ask you to reconsider,' Laura pleaded desperately now as she leapt to her feet to confront him. 'If not for my sake, then for the sake of their child ... don't publicise your theories.'

'My theories are based on certain facts, Mrs DeVere, and it's my job to make my findings public,' he stated adamantly, but he lost a considerable amount of his cockiness when Anton walked into the living-room, but Laura sighed inwardly with relief. She did not know how or why he had come home so early, but the main thing was that he was there.

'If you print any of that drivel, I shall personally sue you *and* your newspaper, but if it's a story you want, then I'll give it to you,' Anton said in a calm, deadly voice that sent an involuntary shiver up Laura's spine as he continued. 'Robert Dean and his wife were on a pleasure cruise, nothing more, and the explosion on board their yacht was caused by an electrical fault which started a fire near the petrol supply tanks. That's all.'

'If that's all, Mr DeVere, then why has this entire incident been shrouded in such secrecy?' Tim Farrell demanded, obviously not in the least convinced.

'There's never been any need for secrecy,' Anton explained. 'It's merely been my intention to shield their daughter from the horror of what actually happened. A violent storm is a hazard to every yachtsman at sea. Their daughter knew this, and I decided that the knowledge that they were shipwrecked in one such storm would be a more acceptable explanation for someone of her age.'

'Is this the truth, Mr DeVere?' Tim Farrell questioned daringly.

'Do you doubt my word?' Anton demanded autocratically, the height and size of him dwarfing the young man considerably.

'How do you explain that Russian trawler docking beside them in Walvis Bay on such a flimsy excuse, and why did the explosion occur at the exact time Robert Dean was to break radio silence?' the reporter continued a little sceptically, and with a boldness Laura had to admire.

'The time of the explosion was a coincidence, nothing more, and the trawler ...' Anton shrugged his broad shoulders beneath the superbly tailored jacket of his dark grey suit and said authoritatively, 'its unscheduled stop was quite innocent. They thought they had a sick man on board, but it turned out they were wrong, and they left at once.'

'It seems I'm not the only one who's been investigating

the accident,' the reporter remarked suspiciously.

'No, Farrell, you're not, and I've heard several other improbable theories from various sensation-seekers such as yourself,' Anton assured him harshly. 'There was no mystery involved in their deaths, as the official investigation proved, so drop the subject, and find yourself a sensational story elsewhere.'

Tim Farrell's face fell. 'There's been an official investigation, then?'

'Naturally,' Anton smiled, but his eyes remained hard and cold. 'If you stop to have a chat to your editor you'll discover that an official report is being prepared for tomorrow's edition of your newspaper, and the contents will be exactly as I told you, except that your editor, along with several others, has kindly agreed not to dwell on the explosion on board the yacht.'

The young man went white, then red as he glanced from Anton to Laura and back again, but anger and defeat was mirrored in his eyes when he said abruptly, 'I'm sorry I wasted your time.'

Anton and Laura faced each other in silence until the outer door closed behind him, then Laura asked jerkily, 'What's the truth, Anton?'

His mouth tightened ominously, then his explanation fell harshly on her ears. 'The Russian trawler and the bomb on board the *Bluebird* is fact, but there's no proof to lay accusations at anyone's door. We're pretty sure, though, that someone must have known that Robert had it in his power to alleviate the oil crisis in South Africa. He had influential friends in the right places who might have sold oil to us at a not so exorbitant price, and this was what our enemies wanted to prevent.'

Laura's aching head was spinning with the effort to assimilate these new facts and, turning from him, she said weakly, 'I think I'll go upstairs, if you don't mind.'

'Before you go,' he said abruptly, reaching the door before her and closing it in a manner that placed her on her guard for some unknown reason, but she understood why the next instant when he asked, 'Who's your friend in Sea Point?'

Laura knew at once that no one but Camilla could have passed this information on to him, and her pulse hammered nervously in her throat as she said with forced casualness, 'It's no one you would know.'

'Is it a man?' he demanded harshly, his eyes glittering hard as they flicked over her.

She shrugged tiredly. 'What difference does it make? I'm entitled to have friends of my own, aren't I?'

'Is he a friend, or a lover?'

'Don't be ridiculous! Alex——' She bit her lip, cursing herself for that slip of the tongue in her moment of anger.

'So it's Alex, is it?' he smiled cynically, lessening the distance between them until he towered over her like a hawk preparing for the kill. 'Alex *who*?'

'It's none of your business!' she snapped furiously, only to find her shoulders gripped in fingers of steel intent on punishment.

'That's where you're wrong, Laura. It's very much my business.' His voice was low and dangerous. 'Do you tell me freely, or do I have to force the truth out of you?'

'You have no right to question me like this,' she protested hotly. 'I don't question your affair with Countess von Dissel, and I——'

'Be very careful what you say, Laura,' he interrupted, his hands biting deeper into the soft flesh of her upper arms, and his nearness a bitter-sweet agony that made her want to weep. 'Now, tell me,' he insisted, his eyes like twin blades piercing her soul. 'Who is this man you've been seeing?'

'His name is Alex Muir,' she relented in fear. 'He's an artist, and he was responsible for the décor of that new business centre in the city.'

'Is he your lover?' he shot the next question at her, making her flinch.

She shook her head dumbly, unable to speak past the lump in her throat.

'*Don't lie to me, damn you!*' he shouted, shaking her until it felt as if her neck would snap.

'I'm *not* lying to you,' she gasped, her head falling forward until her hair veiled the tears on her thick, dark lashes. 'Please, you're h-hurting m-me,' she begged at last, unable to stand the pain a moment longer.

'Do you expect me to believe you went to this man's flat for two days in a row, and that your association with him is purely platonic?' he demanded cynically, slackening his grip on her arms, but not releasing her. 'What do you think I am, Laura? A halfwit?'

She raised her head and stared unwaveringly for a moment into those cold, accusing eyes, then she said with complete honesty, 'I've been going to Alex's flat every morning for the past two weeks.'

'So I'm getting the truth at last, am I?' he grated, his lips drawn back against his teeth in a sneer, then she was released with a suddenness that made her stagger. 'Go on,' he ordered harshly. 'I'm waiting for an explanation.'

'I met Alex once, very briefly, at the start of our holiday at Gordon's Bay, and we met for the second time at the opening of that new business centre.'

'Was that when you both discovered that you had an undying passion for each other?'

Laura felt like slapping him, but she curled her fingers tightly into her palms. 'The only passion Alex has ever displayed in my presence is his passion for art,' she said tritely. 'He's doing a portrait of me.'

'At his suggestion, or yours?' Anton wanted to know, his eyes narrowing.

'It was at his suggestion.'

His mouth curved derisively. 'It's a nude study, no doubt.'

'Just what do you think I am, Anton?' she demanded hoarsely, her eyes sparkling with an inner anger.

'You're my wife, and I forbid you to see this man again,' he stated coldly.

'I'm afraid I have to go for the final sitting tomorrow.'

'Forget it!' Anton thundered, towering over her once more in a way that made her tremble inwardly with renewed fear. 'I will not have people making nasty speculations about my wife!'

'Do you prefer them to make nasty speculations about Camilla and yourself?' Laura countered swiftly in a flash of anger she could not control.

Anton went peculiarly white about the mouth, then one hand encircled her throat, exerting a pressure which almost shut off her supply of air. 'Don't drive me too far, Laura,' he warned savagely. 'You will not see this man again. Do I make myself clear?'

Dizzy, and horrifyingly close to fainting, she said hastily, 'Very clear.'

She was released at once and stood swaying before him for a moment until her head cleared, then, choking back a sob, she wrenched open the door to beat a hasty retreat up to her room.

Dinner was a silent affair that evening, with Anton seated morosely at the head of the table. Sally ventured a questioning glance in Laura's direction, but Laura gestured her unobtrusively to silence, and afterwards they both trouped upstairs without speaking.

Alone in her room once more, Laura supposed it *had* been wrong of her to agree to sit for Alex without Anton knowing, but she felt that Anton was as much to blame for the existing situation. He had openly encouraged Camilla, and had made no secret of the fact that he had preferred her company. Now that her anger and her hurt had subsided, she realised that her visits to Alex's flat could very easily have been interpreted incorrectly. When they saw his flat, of course, they would realise their mistake, but ... Oh, damn!

A car came up the drive, and, thinking it might be Graham, Laura touched up her make-up and went down-

stairs a few minutes later. She heard the low murmur of
Anton's deep-throated voice as she crossed the hall, but it
was Camilla's voice which made her jerk to a halt when she
reached the living-room door.

'Anton darling,' Laura heard her say, 'you really must
try to hurry things along a little.'

'I'm doing my best, Camilla, but it will be soon, I promise you,' Anton replied in a calm, reassuring voice.

'I can't wait,' Camilla sighed.

'Neither can I,' Anton agreed with a hint of impatience
in his voice, and through the chink in the door Laura saw
Camilla move towards Anton, presumably into his arms.

She did not stay to witness more, and, turning blindly,
she made her way upstairs as swiftly as her trembling legs
would allow. When she reached the sanctuary of her bedroom Camilla's 'I can't wait' ricocheted tauntingly through
her mind, and hard at its heels followed Anton's impatient,
'Neither can I.'

'Dear heaven,' she thought as she lowered her trembling
body on to the bed and buried her face in her hands, 'how
much pain and suffering can one person endure before that
stage is reached where it no longer matters?'

Laura slept badly that night, but when she awoke the
following morning she had come to a decision about what
she would do. She was going to Alex's flat for that final
sitting, regardless of what Anton might say or do.

'I'm not supposed to be here,' she told Alex later that
morning as she arranged herself into her usual position on
the low stool near the window.

'Why not?' Alex asked, glancing at her sharply.

'Anton has discovered that I've been coming here,' she
explained, bitterness curving her mouth. 'He thinks we're
having an affair, and has forbidden me to see you again.'

'You shouldn't have kept it a secret from him that you
were coming here to have your portrait painted.'

'Perhaps,' she shrugged carelessly. 'But if he can do just
as he pleases, why can't I?'

'That's a dangerous attitude to adopt with a man like

Anton DeVere,' Alex warned. 'You should know better than I do that he's not the kind of man to accept that type of reasoning.'

'He's selfish, egotistical, arrogant, and——'

'And you love him,' Alex filled in quietly for her when she paused.

For a moment Laura could not speak, then she groaned, 'Oh, God, I wish I were dead!'

'Cheer up, Laura. Things are usually never as bad as they seem,' he reassured her with that flashing smile which usually drew a similar response from her. 'How's the head?'

'It's aching a bit this morning, but I'll survive.'

I'll survive. Her own words echoed back at her hollowly while Alex worked on in silence. She would survive, but she would not have lived. She swallowed down the painful lump in her throat, and stared fixedly out of the window in an effort not to cry, but the restless, turbulent sea offered her no peace of mind, nor the comfort she so desperately needed.

'You can relax, Laura,' Alex said at last, putting down his brushes. 'It's done.'

'May I look now?' she asked eagerly, swinging her legs stiffly to the floor.

'Not yet,' he smiled. 'I still have to add the finishing touches, but for that I regrettably shan't be requiring your delightful presence.'

Laura stared at him for a moment, taking in the sun-bleached hair, and the tall, lanky body clad in old denims and paint-bespattered blue shirt. In a short space of time he had become her friend, and someone she could confide in, she thought, and then she sighed, 'I think I'm going to miss these sessions here with you.'

'I don't think,' he grinned at her ruefully. 'I *know* I'm going to miss not having you here.'

There was something in those hazel eyes; something she

had not seen there before, and she found it flattering as well as disturbing.

'You will let me see the portrait before you exhibit it, won't you?' she changed the subject quickly.

'I won't exhibit it without letting you see it first, nor will I exhibit it without your husband's permission.'

'You don't need permission from Anton,' she stated indignantly.

Alex smiled indulgently, but remained adamant. 'I think it would perhaps be advisable to get his permission.'

'Do as you please,' she sighed at length, and suddenly the shrill peal of the doorbell quivered along her nerves, filling her with an acute sense of danger. 'Alex?'

He looked down at her hand clutching his arm, and covered it briefly with his strong, artistic fingers. 'Take it easy.'

The doorbell pealed again—impatiently this time—and Alex crossed the room to answer it. Anton, formidable and frightening, filled the doorway, and Laura's heart lurched with sickening fear as their eyes met across the space dividing them.

'I've come to collect my wife,' he stated harshly, barely acknowledging Alex as he strode past him in Laura's direction, and suddenly she transgressed beyond the point of fear to a peak of anger which seemed to shake through her like a volcanic eruption.

'I'm not a package in some lost property department which has to be collected, Anton,' she said in a voice that was shaking with the force of her emotions. 'I came here on my own, and I shall leave that way when it suits me.'

'You're coming with me *now*!' he thundered at her, his dominating presence making the room shrivel in size, but Laura refused to be intimidated.

'You have a nerve coming here and ordering me about like this!' she snapped.

'I think you'd better do as your husband suggests, Laura, and go with him,' Alex spoke for the first time, and

Anton turned on him with barely concealed savageness.

'That's sensible advice, Muir,' he said through clenched teeth. 'You might as well know that at this moment I'd like nothing better than to knock your teeth in!'

'Anton!' Laura cried out at once, ashamed as well as angered that he should behave in this manner towards a man who had treated her with nothing but kindness and respect.

'Get your coat,' Anton snapped. 'You're leaving.'

She could almost feel his body vibrating with anger, and one look at the taut, hard line of his jaw made her realise that she would be tempting fate to continue defying him.

She picked up her coat and handbag, and barely had time to apologise to Alex before cruel fingers bit into her arm, and ushered her out to the lift.

What happened afterwards was close to a nightmare. Anton followed her all the way to Bellavista in his Jaguar, travelling so close behind her that she could almost feel him breathing fire down her neck. Her hands were shaking, and twice she stalled the car. On the second occasion, however, Anton climbed out of his Jaguar and strode across to her with quick, angry strides. He jerked open the door at her side, and his fury washed over her like a merciless storm battering the vulnerable coast, and it left her considerably more shaken than before.

Perilously close to tears, she took refuge in anger, and when she finally drove through Bellavista's gates with Anton hot on her trail, she felt more than ready to face him once more.

In the absolute privacy of their bedroom, Laura observed Anton a little warily while he took off his jacket, removed his tie, and undid the top button of his shirt as if it choked him. His movements were jerky with suppressed violence, and despite the angry bitterness churning through her, she had to admire his magnificent physique, and the proud tilt of his head above the broad, powerful shoulders.

The atmosphere was electrifyingly tense between them

when he finally turned on her and demanded harshly, 'Just what did you mean by disobeying my orders?'

'Just what did you mean by barging into Alex's flat and behaving as though I were an errant schoolgirl indulging in an illicit love affair?' she countered angrily.

His nostrils flared. 'I warn you, Laura ...'

'Don't threaten me!' she almost shouted at him, her eyes dark and mutinous. 'I've taken about as much as I can stand from you. Circumstances forced us into this hateful marriage, but that's no reason why you should have treated me as abominably as you have.'

'My God, haven't I given you enough?' he demanded with harsh cynicism. 'I gave you my name, my home, and all the comforts a man in my position could offer the woman he married. What more do you want?'

She clenched her hands at her sides in an effort to stop them from shaking. 'There are other things a woman needs besides that.'

'Such as what, for instance?' Those steely eyes raked her from head to foot with an insulting arrogance which stung deeply. 'Don't tell me that the amount I've been depositing into your banking account isn't enough, or that you haven't derived any satisfaction from my lovemaking.'

'Money and sex!' she spat out the words in disgust. 'Is that *all* you can think of?'

His hand shot out and grasped her wrist, jerking her up against him so that the full fury of his eyes burned down into hers. 'If I find out that you've been seeing that man again, Laura, then I won't be held responsible for my actions.'

'You can't choose my friends for me,' she argued, ignoring the danger signals which flashed persistently through her brain.

Anton's mouth thinned into an ominous line. 'I will not have people suggesting that my wife has a lover tucked away behind my back!'

'What are you afraid of, Anton? That they may suspect

you're impotent?' The words were out before she could prevent them, and when she saw his harsh features darken with the most terrible fury, she knew she had gone too far. 'I'm sorry, Anton,' she said shakily. 'I—I shouldn't have said that.'

'No, you shouldn't have,' he ground out the words through a tightly clenched jaw, 'but now you're going to pay for it!'

There was one sure way that he could punish her, and when the rasping sound of her zip reached her ears she knew exactly what he intended doing to her.

'Anton, I beg of you—*don't*!' she cried hoarsely, but her pleas were futile, and so were her efforts to fight him off while he divested her of her clothes.

Blinded by tears and a stabbing pain at her temples, she was too exhausted to deter him eventually when he carried her across to the bed and dropped her unceremoniously on to it.

'Let's see who's impotent, shall we?' his voice sliced through her, then he flung himself down beside her, and her lips were crushed into submission beneath that cruel, hard mouth.

In his anger Anton showed her no mercy. Not even when she sobbed with misery did he relent, and she was forced to endure his fury until he lay physically spent beside her.

Laura felt exhausted and defeated, but, more than that, she felt humiliated and degraded. There was the taste of gall in her mouth, and an aching despair in her heart while she watched him get up and dress himself. What kind of man was he? she wondered, barely able to conceal the pain in her eyes when he turned to face her. Did he possess no soul, no heart that she could have reached with her own?

His face was an impenetrable mask as he stood looking down at her; a mask carved out of granite the same as his heart, she thought as she searched futilely for the slightest sign of humanity.

'Contrary to what you may think,' he said thickly, his voice shattering the turbulent silence as if he had probed her mind, 'I don't enjoy taking a woman by force, or in anger. To say that I was driven to it is no excuse either. I despise men who lack such obvious control, and if it gives you any satisfaction, then you may as well know that I despise myself more than you ever could at this moment.'

Laura drew a shuddering, faintly incredulous breath, and called out his name, but he had picked up his discarded jacket, and was gone before she could say anything further.

She had never heard him speak like that before, and it troubled her, but as the days passed and lengthened into a week, she found herself unable to penetrate the barrier of cold indifference which he erected between them whenever they met, and through it all there was the agony of expecting to be told at any moment that he wanted to end their marriage.

One evening, at the dinner table, Sally ventured to ask if they had quarrelled with each other, only to be told sharply by Anton to mind her own business. Afterwards, Sally had lapsed into a brooding silence which merely added to Laura's problems. Children were quick to sense an atmosphere in the home, and Sally, more than anyone else, needed to be protected from it. Laura shuddered at the thought of how Sally would react to the news that the two people she loved most were separating.

'Sally will just have to learn to adapt herself to circumstances,' Gina stated firmly when Laura confided in her the following morning. 'I never thought Anton would allow Camilla to get her claws into him again,' Gina added distastefully, 'and it just goes to show that even the cleverest men are not above behaving like fools where a woman like that is concerned.'

'Gina ... about that evening when you came to dinner ...' Laura began, but Gina gestured her to silence.

'Forget it, my dear,' she smiled, then her glance became thoughtful. 'Have you seen the morning papers?'

'No,' Laura shook her head warily. 'Anton must have taken them to the office with him.'

'Avron Enterprises has been sold,' Gina supplied the information which shook Laura's foundations considerably. 'The name of the buyer is being withheld until all the necessary papers have been drawn up.'

Laura was not certain how this would affect her, but she felt dismally sure that she would not have long to wait to find out.

That same evening after dinner, Anton surprised Laura by following her into the living-room, but he sat reading his newspaper in stony silence in front of the log fire while she tried desperately to concentrate on a magazine. Outside it continued to rain steadily, as it had done since early that afternoon, and the cold dampness of that winter night made her draw closer to the fire.

'How much longer?' she wondered distractedly. 'How much longer do I have to wait for Anton to tell me of his intention to marry Camilla?'

The doorbell chimed unexpectedly, interrupting her thoughts, and moments later Eddie appeared in the living-room door. 'A Mr Muir to see you, Mr Anton.'

Laura looked up with a start and glanced in swift fear at her husband, but his face remained expressionless as he said: 'Send him in.'

Eddie disappeared, and seconds later Alex entered the living-room carrying a large, carefully wrapped package in his hands.

'Good evening,' he smiled with a cheerfulness Laura wished she could match as she and Anton rose to their feet simultaneously.

'To what do we owe the pleasure of this visit?' Anton asked with thinly veiled sarcasm, but Alex remained unconcerned.

'I need your permission to exhibit this portrait of Laura at the National Art Gallery tomorrow,' he explained, gesturing to the large object in his hands.

There was a brief, tense silence before Anton said abruptly, 'I shall have to see it first.'

'Certainly,' Alex agreed, placing the portrait on a low table against the wall and removing the canvas wrapping with great care. 'Behold!' he said at last with a certain amount of drama as he removed the final covering. 'You're witnessing the unveiling of a masterpiece.'

Laura drew an audible breath as she found herself staring at the portrait of herself seated on the rocks at Gordon's Bay with her honey-brown hair blowing free behind her. It was a magnificent work of art, she realised at once, but she stared at her image as if she were seeing herself for the first time; a serene stranger with a tender yet faintly provocative smile hovering about the soft curve of her mouth. The most striking part, however, was the deep blue eyes. Heavily fringed with dark lashes, they looked out across the turbulent sea with a mysterious mixture of sadness and longing, and quite suddenly Laura could not bear to look at it for a moment longer. It felt as if her soul had been stripped bare to be placed there on canvas for the world to see. It was shattering—terrifying—and she dared not imagine what Anton must be thinking.

'What do you think, Mr DeVere?' Alex unsuspectingly echoed her thoughts, and she glanced fearfully at Anton, but she saw only his austere profile, and that angry nerve pulsing in his cheek. 'Do I have your permission to exhibit this portrait of your wife?' Alex asked.

Anton's unfathomable glance captured Laura's for several breathtaking seconds before he turned to Alex and said roughly, 'It would be an injustice not to exhibit it.'

'I knew you'd feel that way,' Alex smiled with satisfaction, glancing at Laura, who had not spoken since his arrival. 'You haven't given your opinion, Laura.'

'Alex, I—I don't know what to say,' she began lamely. 'It's magnificent, but——' She saw him raise his eyebrows questioningly and added almost accusingly, 'You made me look beautiful.'

'No,' Alex shook his head. 'I painted you the way God created you. It's the true image no mirror will ever produce for you, for no one is ever capable of seeing themselves as they really are.'

'How much do you want for the portrait?'

Laura sucked her breath in sharply and stared incredulously at Anton as Alex said quite distinctly, 'It's not for sale, Mr DeVere.'

'You're throwing away a fortune,' Anton accused angrily. 'I'm insisting that you name your price, and whatever it is, I'll pay it.'

Was she hearing correctly? Laura wondered confusedly. Was Anton actually offering to buy that portrait of herself?

'This portrait is not mine to sell, Mr DeVere,' Alex insisted calmly, and Laura glanced sharply at the tall, lanky artist. She had the most alarming suspicion that she was about to be exposed, and she tried frantically to catch Alex's eye, but he kept his glance resolutely fixed on Anton. 'This portrait is my gift to Laura,' he continued, 'and she will eventually give it to the man she loves.'

Laura wished suddenly that the floor would open up beneath her, but nothing of the sort happened, and she stood there, petrified, and terrifyingly aware of the dark fury on every line of Anton's face.

'I presume you're referring to yourself when you speak of the man she loves?' Anton demanded harshly, and Laura shrank inwardly from this nightmare situation.

Was Alex trying to destroy her? He knew she loved Anton. Did he intend to make her suffer the most painful humiliation of all by divulging the secret she had entrusted to him? 'Oh, God! Please! *Please!*' she prayed silently, her palms cold and clammy as she clenched them at her sides.

'I was not referring to myself,' Alex replied in a totally undisturbed manner, but his eyes glittered with that peculiar alertness she had noticed so often before. 'I admit I would give anything for that to be so,' he added, 'but Laura's heart belongs elsewhere, and I must join the ranks

of those who admire from afar.' Laura felt as if her mind
was in the grip of a vice which was being tightened mercilessly as she watched Alex wrap the portrait meticulously
before he turned to face her with a smile which was oddly
reassuring under the circumstances. 'You shall have this
portrait, Laura, as soon as my exhibition closes, and you
will naturally receive an invitation for two to attend the
opening tomorrow.' He paused, smiled again, then picked
up the portrait and left with a brief, 'Goodnight.'

CHAPTER TEN

A STONY silence followed Alex's departure; a silence which lingered on until they heard his car going down the drive, and only then did Anton stir.

'If it's not Alex Muir,' he said in that dangerously quiet voice she knew so well, 'then who is this man you're supposed to be in love with?'

'Alex is m-mistaken,' she stammered. 'There's no one.'

'You're lying to me, Laura.'

'No, no!' she denied anxiously, backing away as he approached her.

'Then who do you want to give that portrait to?'

'No one,' she cried, her temples drumming until it felt as though she would go mad. 'I don't want to give it to anyone!'

'Dammit, Laura, I demand to know the truth!' Anton thundered at her, his face distorted with the fury that raged through him as he lunged at her.

'No, no, stay away from me!' she begged desperately, stumbling in her effort to escape him, but steely fingers snaked about her arm, and she was dragged up against him until his eyes, like blue flames, burned down into hers with a probing intensity which frightened her.

'Tell me!' he demanded through his teeth. 'Who is this man?'

'I can't tell you,' she cried almost hysterically, her eyes wide and dark in her ashen face. 'Please . . . I can't'

A terrible look came into his eyes, and fear such as she had never known before shook through her when he said gratingly, 'So you admit that there *is* someone.'

'No!' she screamed hoarsely, then something seemed to snap in her mind, and, with an unexpected burst of strength

168

which she had not known she possessed, she broke free of him and fled, shouting, 'Leave me alone, I can't stand much more of this!'

'Laura, come back here!' he commanded sharply, but she had already darted through the front door and out into the dark, rainy night as if the devil himself was after her.

She was soaked to the skin in seconds, and chilled to the marrow, but she paused only once in the blind urgency of her flight to sum up the situation. She had a choice; the treacherous mountain ahead of her. She heard his harsh, commanding voice call out to her, and chose the mountain like a frightened animal.

'Oh, God, let me die!' she begged in an anguished voice. 'Just let me die!'

She was stumbling over rocks and protruding roots, frantically following the steep path for what seemed an eternity until she found her way barricaded by a wire fence. A few feet below her she could hear Anton approaching. He shouted a warning, but she was deaf to everything except the mad desire to escape the humiliation of having to face him with the truth.

The barbed wire ripped at her hands when she climbed over it into the prohibited area and, with her breath rasping painfully in her throat, she continued her flight, only vaguely aware that the ground had levelled out beneath her feet.

'Wait!' a voice warned urgently after she had barely gone a few paces. 'Don't go any further!'

Laura came to an abrupt halt and glanced over her shoulder, but there was no one there except the rain and the eerie darkness, and she shivered uncontrollably. Was she going mad? Could that warning voice have been her own conscience, or had she actually heard a strange woman's voice urging her not to go further? 'Ridiculous,' she told herself with a hysterical laugh.

'Laura, for God's sake come away there,' Anton's voice warned urgently when she was about to go on. 'You're on the edge of an almost vertical cliff,' he added, making her aware of the danger ahead.

The rain lashed her body while she stood frozen with indecision. Should she go on to whatever lay before her, or should she return to be taunted for loving unwisely?

'I can't bear it!' she cried tiredly, her tears mingling with the rain on her face as she turned to glance at Anton's tall, dark frame where he stood motionless on the other side of the fence. 'I just can't bear it!' she repeated, swaying away from him.

'Take it easy, Laura,' Anton said quickly in a voice that sounded oddly raw. 'If you go much further you—you'll *kill* yourself.'

Kill yourself! Kill yourself! The words echoed through her tortured mind until she wanted to scream. 'You can't kill yourself,' the voice of her conscience warned unexpectedly. 'You can't take an innocent child with you to your grave because you're a coward. He deserves to grow inside you, and to live.'

She shuddered as she came to her senses. She had gone a little crazy, but she had never been a coward and, silently, she walked towards the fence where Anton awaited her. He lifted her over it without a word, but when she stood before him, shivering and wet to the skin, the full realisation of what she had contemplated struck her like a physical blow. 'Logical, sensible Laura,' her sister had always called her, and she groaned inwardly, 'Oh, Elizabeth, if only you could see me now!'

She choked on a sob and, not caring what Anton thought of her, she flung herself against his equally wet body and clung to him while she wept unrestrainedly.

His arms went about her at once, and he held her so tightly when her tears subsided that she began to think he had saved her from falling down the cliff only to crush her to death. She felt him shaking, just as she was shaking, while they stood there on the dark mountain with the rain pelting down on them, then he lifted her in his arms like a child and carried her back to the house as he had done once before.

'Take a hot bath, and get into bed,' he ordered abruptly when he had lowered her to her feet in their bedroom, and Laura obeyed meekly.

She soaked herself for a considerable time before the chill left her body entirely, then she dried herself vigorously and did the same with her hair before she slipped into the pink, frilly nightdress which she had worn for the first time on their wedding night. Their wedding night! she thought tiredly as she climbed into bed and slipped beneath the warm blankets. An eternity seemed to have passed since that night when she had submitted to Anton in fear and had emerged ecstatic the morning after. An eternity, yet it was not quite four months ago.

The door opened, interrupting her thoughts, and Anton walked in. He had changed, she noticed distractedly, into a pale green shirt and dark green suede pants which were fastened about his lean hips with an ostrich skin belt. Laura felt his eyes on her, but she could not look at him as he approached the bed, and not even when he sat down beside her to examine the scratches on her hands could she find the courage to raise her eyes to his. His thumbs moved lightly against her palms, sending a tingling sensation up her arms as she waited for him to speak, to demand once again that she should give him the name of the man she loved.

'Oh, Anton, Anton, if only you knew—but I dare not tell you,' she sighed inwardly.

His thumbs ceased their caressing movements as he gripped her hands tightly, and she looked up suddenly, straight into those steel-grey eyes. He looked white and drawn, and his eyes had a feverish look about them that disturbed her deeply. He opened his mouth to say something, but seemingly couldn't, and her concern changed to fear.

Was it his freedom he was about to ask for? she wondered as she whispered hoarsely, 'What is it, Anton?'

He continued to stare at her for nerve-racking seconds as if he had not heard, then he groaned from deep within his throat and gathered her into his arms, their hard strength crushing her against him with the same ferocity he had displayed up there on the mountain.

Surprised and bewildered, she remained taut in his embrace as he buried his face against her throat, then, almost as if the words were torn from him by force, he muttered thickly, 'God, Laura, I love you!'

It seemed as though the air in her lungs, which had survived the crushing pressure of his arms, had suddenly deserted her. This had to be part of a mad, crazy dream; a figment of her imagination which stemmed from the desperate need in her heart. It was too incredible to believe; too frighteningly wonderful to grasp, and yet he had uttered the words he had sworn never to use. Could she believe it? Dared she?

'Why aren't you laughing?' he groaned, and she could feel his warm breath against her throat as he spoke. 'Why aren't you laughing as you once threatened you would?'

A great surge of joy swept through her, filling her eyes with tears, and making them glitter like blue sapphires as she placed a gentle hand on either side of his head and brought his face out into the open.

'The laughter will come later, Anton,' she said unsteadily, looking up into his wary eyes. 'This is the terrifying moment of truth.'

'What's so terrifying about the truth?'

'I wanted to die rather than hear you laugh at me for admitting that it's *you* I love,' she said simply.

He stared at her in solemn silence, his eyes probing hers with a burning intensity as she raised the shutters, then he was seeing down into the very depths of her soul.

'Laura, Laura,' he muttered thickly, his fingers brushing her hair lightly from her flushed cheeks while his eyes de-

voured her. 'God knows I've never felt more humble than
at this moment.'

'It doesn't suit you to be humble, my proud, arrogant beloved,' she laughed softly through her tears. 'Just kiss me,
and tell me again that you love me, and ... Oh, Anton,
hold me tight!'

His arms were hard about her, threatening her ribs with
extinction, but she did not care. He buried his lips in the
silky fragrance of her hair, and trailed them across her
throat and smooth cheek until he covered her eager, tremu-
lous mouth with his own. He kissed her with a tender
passion which stirred her more deeply than anything had
ever done before, and her arms tightened about his neck
while she lost herself in the wonder of that moment. But
in every paradise there was a serpent to intrude on moments
such as this, and she drew away from him.

'What about Camilla?' she asked hesitantly.

His mouth hardened into a thin line as he said : 'I think
we've just about seen the last of her.'

She did not pretend to understand as she asked, 'Was
she to blame for the way you felt about women?'

'Not entirely,' he smiled with the old familiar cynicism
as he released her and lit a cigarette. 'The DeVere men
have never been lucky in their choice of women. My grandfather used to say the DeVeres were cursed because of
Friedrich acquiring his wealth, *and* Bellavista, by card-
sharping people out of their money and possessions.'

'But that's ridiculous!'

'When you hear what I have to say you might not think
so,' he frowned down at her, drawing hard on his cigarette.
'It started with Friedrich when Dora walked out on him.'

'No one can swear to that, because no one knows for sure
what happened to her.'

'Then my great-grandmother was afflicted with insanity.'

'She probably never was a mentally strong person, and
Friedrich's death, following Dora's disappearance, merely
tipped the scales for her,' Laura interrupted once again, but

Anton continued as if she had not spoken.

'My grandmother died when my father was born . . .'

'That happened often in those days when medical knowledge was still so limited.'

'. . . and my mother ran out on my father and myself when I was five.'

Laura's compassionate heart felt the pain that must have been his once, and her eyes filled with tears.

'No clever repartee this time?' Anton demanded with that faintly mocking smile she knew so well, and, when she shook her head, his expression hardened. 'My father's bitterness washed over on to me, and, with my grandfather filling my mind with the family history, it was enough to put me off marriage for life.' He smoked his cigarette in angry silence for a time before he continued. 'As for Camilla, she came into my life at a time when my father's health was waning, and he wanted to see me married despite everything he'd suffered. Camilla was persuasive, and I was on the verge of thinking marriage a good idea when my father died. He left behind a business which had become a liability rather than an asset, and Camilla retreated smartly when she heard the news, but Karl von Dissel became her willing victim.'

'And your faith in women took a further plunge,' Laura added quietly.

'Women are good for only one thing,' he said harshly, putting out his cigarette and staring hard at her. 'Am I a fool to think I can trust you, Laura?'

'If we can't trust each other, then there's no point in continuing with our marriage.'

He raised her hand to his lips and she felt them burning against her palm. 'Do *you* trust *me*?'

'I know I went a little crazy this evening, but yes . . .' She smiled tremulously. 'I would trust you with my life.'

'My darling!' he sighed a little unsteadily, almost as if he had been holding his breath, then she was in his arms and they were kissing each other a little wildly until Anton

lowered her back on to the pillows with a smile that softened his features in a way she had never seen before. 'Stay
here,' he said. 'I'll make you something warm to drink.'

'Anton ...' she caught at his hand before he could get
up, 'don't be long.'

His lips brushed against hers, travelled across her cheek
to her throat, and returned once more to her lips. 'I'll be
as quick as I can.'

Laura sighed contentedly as the door closed behind him,
and smiled. There was so much they still had to talk about,
and so much she still did not understand, but knowing that
she was loved was of more importance than anything else.

Her thoughts returned to that moment on the mountain
when she had stood poised on the edge of the cliff. She had
known that the fenced-off area was forbidden, but she had
never known why. For a few mad moments she had considered death, yes, but she shuddered to think what would
have happened if that voice had not warned her to stop. It
had been so real, that voice in the rain, but it could not
have been. In a flash of sanity she must have had a pre-
monition of the danger lurking at her feet, and that voice
could only have sprung from her own thoughts. It was a
logical conclusion to reach, but it still troubled her.

The sound of a car coming up the drive intruded into
her thoughts, but she sat for some time listening to the
rain beating against the windows before she got out of bed
and pulled on her gown to go in search of Anton. Whom,
or what, was keeping him so long? she wondered.

She could distinguish the low murmur of his voice
when she crossed the hall a few minutes later in her soft
slippers, but as she approached the living-room door the
sound of a feminine voice made all her old fears return with
a rush, and a coldness swept through her that made her
freeze just inside the door.

Camilla was raising her glass to her sensuous mouth, and
she sipped carefully at her Martini before she smiled at
Anton with a mixture of confidence and disbelief.

'You surely don't expect me to take you seriously?'

'I am serious, Camilla,' Anton said, his jaw hard and unrelenting. 'Find someone else to lean on.'

'But, darling, you know how much I rely on you, and besides ...' She put down her glass and placed a beautiful, slender hand on his arm as she added a little huskily, 'You know you love me, and always will.'

'Love was never what I felt for you, Camilla, even though I once considered marrying you,' Anton stated with a ruthless honesty that drove some of the chill from Laura's heart as she watched him remove Camilla's hand from his arm. 'It took a woman like Laura to teach me the real meaning of the word.'

There was a frightening little silence, then Camilla's laughter jarred Laura's nerves. 'Don't be silly, darling,' she said caustically. 'You can't possibly love that insipid creature.'

'Laura could never be insipid even if she tried,' Anton corrected her harshly. 'She possesses a warmth and sincerity which is enviable, and in every other respect, Camilla, she's by far your superior.' He turned suddenly and saw Laura standing in the doorway. 'Come in, darling,' he smiled, holding out his hand to her. 'Countess von Dissel was just leaving.'

With her confidence restored, Laura went quickly to his side, and she was thankful for that strong, possessive arm he placed about her waist when Camilla's dark, venomous eyes raked her from head to foot before she returned her attention to Anton.

'You can't treat me like this and think you can get away with it!' she spat out the words.

'Can't I?' Anton smiled derisively.

'You know that when I sign those papers tomorrow Avron Enterprises will be mine and, with the von Dissel money behind it, I could ruin you.'

'With *my* money behind it, you mean,' Anton corrected harshly. 'The necessary papers were signed this morning, and Avron Enterprises has now become a subsidiary company of DeVere Enterprises.'

A shock of surprise rippled through Laura, but she was more concerned at that moment with Camilla, whose beautiful face went almost purple with rage.

'You fiend!' Camilla shouted when she managed to find her voice. 'You knew I——'

'Yes, I knew you wanted to buy the company, and I went along with your plans, making you believe that I was negotiating on your behalf while in actual fact I was doing so for myself.' A cynical smile curved his hard mouth. 'You wanted me to sign security for you until Karl's estate was wound up, and I agreed, but while you were congratulating yourself on your easy victory, I was having you investigated.'

'How dare you have me investigated as though I were some sort of criminal!' Camilla shouted at him, but Anton continued as if she had not spoken.

'I received a report yesterday, and I found it extremely interesting to discover that the bulk of Karl von Dissel's estate went to his children by his first marriage.'

'Karl was a fool!'

'*You* were a fool, Camilla, to think you could get away with it,' Anton contradicted icily. 'Or did you think I would merely pay up and smile if you could get me to divorce Laura and marry you before I found out the truth?'

'Even if you hadn't married me I would have repaid every cent once the business was on its feet,' Camilla argued.

'Really?' Anton smiled disdainfully. 'If you'd told me the truth at the start I might have considered assisting you in starting a business, but you lied to me, so what guarantee did I have that you would have repaid me?'

Seeing Camilla with her composure shattered, Laura could almost feel sorry for her, but Camilla rallied swiftly.

'Surely you could have trusted me?' she demanded accusingly.

'Trusted you?' Anton laughed scornfully. 'You married Karl for money and position. Now you have nothing except a meagre yearly allowance and a title which is of no value in this country, so find some other fool to give you the wealth you desire.'

'You're no better than I am!' she shrieked, realising that she had lost, and the woman Laura had once thought beautiful became ugly as she shed completely her cloak of poised dignity. 'You tricked me right from the start!' she flung at Anton accusingly.

'Yes,' he admitted. 'You see, Camilla, I was one jump ahead of you all the time, but now the time for playing games is over, and I sincerely hope our paths never cross in future.'

'You're a fiend! A cruel, insensitive, hateful *fiend*!' Camilla's lips were drawn back against her teeth in a snarl of rage, her dark eyes shooting venomous darts as she turned on Laura and shouted, 'You're *welcome* to him, do you hear?'

Laura flinched when she heard the front door slam behind Camilla moments later, and then she felt Anton shaking with silent laughter beside her. She stared up at him in stern, disapproving silence, but his infectious laughter, like a low rumble in his throat, finally made the corners of her mouth lift in a smile.

'She's right, you know. You *are* a fiend,' she accused, turning into his arms. 'The nicest possible fiend, though.'

'You're prejudiced,' he told her, tongue in cheek.

'Naturally,' she admitted, drawing his head down to hers. 'I love you, remember?'

Their lips met in a long, satisfying kiss that left her flushed and breathless, and with eyes glittering as if the stars had settled in them.

'You should be upstairs in bed waiting like a good girl for your cocoa,' Anton admonished her lightly while his lips trailed tantalisingly from her cheek to her throat.

'I know,' she whispered happily, 'but I heard a car com-

ing up the drive, and when you stayed away so long I wondered if something was wrong.'

'Laura ...' His lips lingered for a moment where he
could feel the rapid beat of her pulse at the base of her
throat, then he raised his head and looked down at her with
something close to remorse in his eyes. 'I must have hurt
you very much at times with my reluctance to explain my
motives for encouraging Camilla, but I would like you to
know that, despite what the newspapers said, our meetings
were purely business, and we were seldom alone, as those
clever photographers tried to imply.'

Laura winced inwardly at the memory of that evening
when he had invited Camilla home for dinner, but she
brushed it aside and smiled. 'We won't talk about it again.'

'No, we won't talk about it again,' he said sternly. 'We'll
talk instead about the child you're going to have, shall we?'

Laura drew a sharp breath and stared up at him with a
measure of uncertainty mirrored in her eyes. 'You know?'

'Did you think I wouldn't?'

'But how?'

He smiled then, and a wave of heat swept up into her
face when he said: 'I haven't been married to you for four
months without learning certain things about you.'

Unable to sustain his glance, she buried her hot face
against him. 'Do you mind? About the baby, I mean?'

'Not if it pleases you to have my child,' he said simply,
and she flung her arms about his neck in a wild surge of
happiness.

'Oh, Anton, Anton, I love you so much!'

His arms tightened about her, and he kissed her hard
and lingeringly on the mouth before he released her. 'I'll
make you a fresh mug of cocoa.'

'I don't really want anything to drink,' she said unsteadily, her heartbeats quickening when she noticed a
wicked gleam in those steel-grey eyes.

'What do you want, then?'

'You,' she said impishly, then she was swung up into his arms.

'You little witch,' he muttered laughingly, then she was being carried from the living-room and up the stairs to their bedroom.

Sally forestalled them in the passage, however, and demanded suspiciously, 'What's wrong with Aunty Laura?'

'Your Aunty Laura has a fever,' Anton announced without hesitation, and Laura flushed hotly.

'Don't be silly, Anton,' she whispered admonishingly, trying to free herself, but his arms merely tightened about her, and a teasing intimacy lurked in the eyes that met hers.

'That's what you said downstairs, wasn't it?' he demanded with mock innocence, and as her colour heightened he turned his attention to Sally. 'By the way,' he told her, 'in a few months' time, if all goes well, we're going to have a baby for you to look after.'

'Really?' Sally demanded, her bright, eager eyes seeking Laura's. 'Really, Aunty Laura?'

'Yes, really,' Laura confirmed weakly.

'Oh, boy!' Sally announced with glee. 'Just wait till I tell the kids at school!'

'Heaven help me,' Laura moaned under her breath.

'What do you want, Uncle Anton?' Sally demanded. 'A boy or a girl?'

'It will be a boy,' he said at once, then his expression grew stern. 'Now get to bed, young lady, and go to sleep.'

'Okay,' Sally agreed obediently. 'Goodnight.'

'Now, where were we?' Anton asked of no one in particular when Sally disappeared into her room.

'Anton ...' Laura began warningly.

'Oh, yes,' he said abruptly, walking with firm, purposeful steps towards their bedroom and kicking the door shut behind him. 'I have to do something about your fever, if I remember correctly.'

'Anton, what if it's a girl?' she asked helplessly as he set her on her feet and removed her nightdress in between kisses.

'Then it will be a delightful change after three generations of boys,' he smiled, drawing her against him, and after that she had no further opportunity to discuss that particular subject.

Their desire for each other was intense and, for the first time, Laura held nothing back. She gave as much as she received during those moments of prolonged pleasure until the exquisite tension snapped within her, and she was submerged in a wave of ecstasy that made her cling to Anton weakly.

Content and happy, she lay in his arms with her head pillowed on his shoulder. Could this be true? Or had it all been a dream? she wondered as she lay listening to the rhythmic beat of his heart. She was pleasantly tired, but she could not sleep, and somehow she sensed that Anton too was lying awake.

His skin was warm and faintly damp when she moved her hand across his hair-roughened chest. 'Darling . . .'

'Hm . . .?' He turned his head and brushed his lips against her forehead.

'When did you know you loved me?'

He laughed softly as he turned to her and trailed a light, caressing hand down along her thigh and up again to cup her breast. 'I think I must have known the very first time I met you.'

'I don't believe you,' she said, staying his hand as it moved downwards once more across her stomach. 'You ignored me so completely that I felt like an intruder on that one occasion when I came here to Bellavista with Robert and Elizabeth.'

'You *were* an intruder,' he agreed instantly. 'You intruded into my waking and sleeping thoughts to such an extent that I became determined to keep you out. Fortunately a distance of over fourteen hundred kilometres separated us, and I made a point of staying out of the way when you came down to Cape Town on your occasional visits, but fate eventually threw us together, and I knew then that I wanted you. I tried to think of a way to keep you here, and Sally's hysterical obsession finally offered the solution to my problem.'

'Marriage,' she concluded with a sigh, recalling how frightened she had been at the prospect of marrying this man she now loved so much.

'Marriage, yes,' Anton repeated. 'Graham practically suggested it, and although I found the idea as distasteful as you did at the time, I knew it would be the only way I could have you.'

'How you must have hated me!'

'Hate is a very strong word,' he said after a thoughtful pause. 'I disliked what you were doing to me, it made me feel uncomfortable, but I wanted you and, as a result, I disliked myself a little bit more each time I made love to you. I tried to stay away from home as much as possible, but when you were at Gordon's Bay with Sally I knew I had to find some excuse to go with you. I remembered your birthday, and rushed out there like an excited schoolboy at the first available opportunity.' He groaned suddenly and buried his face against her throat. 'My behaviour sickened me at times, but I couldn't help myself.'

'Those few days together at the cottage,' Laura whispered, sliding her fingers lovingly through his crisp, dark hair, and pressing her lips against his temple. 'They were something special, weren't they?'

'You certainly made them so.'

'I was trying to show you, in the only way I thought you would understand, that I loved you, but when we returned to Bellavista everything somehow settled back into the same unhappy pattern.'

'Camilla had come back,' he said with the old harshness in his voice. 'When she contacted me a few hours after her arrival, I knew I had to do something about her ... and quickly. It didn't take me long to discover what she was up to, and when she became interested in Avron Enterprises, her motives for looking me up became crystal clear. She was power-hungry, and she wanted it either through me, or through a company of her own. She knew she couldn't succeed either way without me, so she turned on the old charm, and I pretended to fall for it in order to teach her a lesson she wouldn't forget in a hurry.'

'I understand, although I don't entirely approve,' Laura whispered into the darkness. 'I could have murdered both you and Camilla that night you invited her to dinner, and then you still had the gall to stay away hours before you returned home, reeking of her perfume.'

'That was quite a night, one way and another,' Anton laughed mockingly as he kissed her hard on the mouth, then he seemed to sober, and she felt him grow tense beside her in the darkness. 'God, Laura, you've certainly brought out the best and the worst in me since we've been married, and I'll never forget that night when I searched the mountain for you. I knew then what Friedrich must have felt like when he searched for his Dora, and if I'd found you dead, they could have buried me as well.'

'Anton . . .' She tried to speak, but couldn't, and instead she held him close with all the strength in her slender arms.

'I can't tell you what I felt like when I found you lying there in the mist,' he groaned against her breast.

'Why didn't you say something when you came in to see me later that night?'

'I tried to, but you seemed determined to offer me my freedom, so I took myself off and drove about for hours in a reckless fury.'

So it had not been Camilla he had rushed off to in such a hurry, she realised as he switched on the light and lit a cigarette.

'Afterwards,' he went on, blowing a cloud of smoke towards the ceiling, 'when I heard about your visits to Alex

Muir's flat, I thought I'd discovered the reason for your desire to be free.'

'What idiots we've been!' she sighed.

'Alex Muir has a very discerning eye. It was all there in the portrait, and it's here before me now.' There was an unmistakable light in his eyes as he looked down into hers. 'Why have you never looked at me like this before?'

'How could I bare my soul to you when you'd made it so clear that you had no need of my love? That you had only contempt for it, and that—in your own words—you never wanted your intelligence insulted by the mention of the word "love" between us?'

'I recall that incident.' Anton's jaw hardened at the memory. 'It was on our wedding night. You'd said you hated me, and, *dammit*, it had hurt coming from you while I was feeling like an utter cad after having taken you by force.'

Laura trailed coaxing fingers along the hard line of his jaw. 'None of it matters now.'

He turned his lips into her palm, and the tightness left his mouth as they sat in silence for a time, then he sighed and put out his cigarette.

'Laura ...' he began, and for the first time since she had known him, he seemed to be having difficulty in saying what was on his mind.

'You don't have to be afraid to tell me you love me,' she told him gently, and when the look in his eyes told her that she had guessed correctly, she added: 'There are no traps I want to set for you, and no chains to bind you, or limit you in any way which you might find tiresome.'

His strong hands framed her face lightly, and there was a new warmth and tenderness in his glance that made her feel weak with happiness. 'I'm not too proud to admit defeat,' he said, his voice deepening with emotion. 'You've made it possible for me to tell the whole world that I love you, and I shall welcome whatever chains your small hands may desire to place on me, but don't ever go up into the mountain alone again.' His eyes became haunted. 'If you'd fallen down that cliff——'

She silenced him swiftly with her fingers against his lips. 'Forgive me,' she begged softly, then she could no longer delay the questions which were crowding her mind. 'Anton, tell me about that cliff. Are there any ledges or crevices below it?'

'There's a deep crevice about fifteen metres down,' he replied frowningly. 'Why do you ask?'

'If someone fell down there——'

'For God's sake, Laura!'

'No, listen,' she pleaded urgently. 'Is it possible that someone could fall into that crevice and remain undetected?'

Anton's frown deepened. 'It's possible, I suppose, but I fail to see why that should interest you.'

'Would you do something for me, Anton? Would you have that crevice investigated?' He sat up slowly and stared at her incredulously, but before he could question her, she added quickly, 'Don't ask for an explanation now, but would you do it for me?'

She thought for a moment he would refuse, then he nodded slowly, and smiled down at her with tolerant amusement lurking in his eyes. 'If it's important to you . . . yes.'

'Thank you, darling,' she smiled excitedly, the endearment slipping naturally off her lips as she flung her arms about his neck, and kissed him on the mouth, but when she would have drawn away, she found herself held there and kissed with a lingering, deepening passion that found a swift response in her.

Three days later a small party of experienced climbers came down the mountain to report their findings to Laura, and soon after their departure she telephoned Anton at the office to ask him to return home a little earlier that evening.

'You asked me once for proof that Dora hadn't walked out on Friedrich,' she said when they eventually faced each other in the living-room, and in the hand she extended to-

wards him lay a faintly tarnished, heart-shaped gold locket
with the name 'Dora' engraved on the face of it. 'This was
found up there in the crevice, together with what remained
of her body.'

Anton examined the locket in silence, and there was an
odd whiteness about his mouth when he asked, 'What made
you suspect there was something up there?'

A nervous little smile plucked at her lips. 'If I tell you,
will you promise not to laugh?'

He nodded silently, and then Laura told him about that
night when she had imagined she had heard a voice warning her not to go further, and how, after questioning about
the cliff, she had begun to suspect that Dora's body had
remained undiscovered in the crevice.

A long, tense silence followed her disclosure, then Anton
opened his arms wide, and she went into them swiftly to
bury her face against his broad chest.

'We'll bury what's left of Dora alongside Friedrich, and
perhaps now his soul will rest as it should,' Anton murmured almost reverently against her temple, and she
nodded, tears filling her eyes and spilling over on to her
cheeks to dampen his shirt as she pressed closer to him.

The shadows passed on like the seasons and, as Jemima had
predicted, Laura's son was born when the grapes, swollen
with sweetness, were harvested in the valley, and now, at
the age of five months, he already showed signs of possessing a will as strong as his father's, as well as a smile
which could quite likely disarm the devil himself.

From the window of the master bedroom they could see
Sally and Jemima pushing little Friedrich in his pram
through the sun-drenched garden, and their eyes followed
the trio adoringly until they were out of sight.

Laura sighed then, and turned in her husband's arm
to glance up at him with a tender smile hovering on her lips.
An answering smile lurked in the depths of those heavy-
lidded eyes, and the hard mouth softened. That core of

ruthlessness was still there, and so also that immense vitality which was so much a part of his tall, muscular frame. Anton relaxed more often, shedding the pressure of work to become less strained, and, although his cynicism was still clearly evident at times, she had discovered a gentle side to him which few people ever saw. She felt privileged, special, and eternally grateful to be able to share his life.

He brushed the long strands of silky hair away from her face and placed his thumbs beneath her chin so that she was forced to meet the soul-searching penetration of his eyes. 'I have no words to tell you how much I love you.'

'Nor I to tell you how happy it makes me to hear you say that,' she sighed, thrilling to his touch as he slid his hands down her back and drew her closer to the familiar hard length of his body.

'Do we really need words?' he asked against her lips.

'No,' she smiled, then his mouth was plundering hers, and his hands were igniting a flame of desire within her that made her blood flow swiftly and strongly through her veins as he edged her towards the bed and followed her down on to it.

Her fingers tightened in his hair as she drew his head down invitingly on to her breast, but it was when she felt him tremble against her that she knew this man would be hers until the seasons no longer came and went in the valley.

Harlequin Plus

A WORD ABOUT THE AUTHOR

Yvonne Whittal's childhood was spent in Port Elizabeth, on the southern tip of Africa. She recalls dreaming of the day she would be able to travel to unknown countries.

At a very early age she began scribbling stories. Her ambition to be a writer resurfaced after her marriage and the birth of three daughters. She enrolled in a writing course, began submitting short stories to publishers and, with each rejection letter, became all the more determined.

Turning to the task of writing a full-length book, Yvonne was encouraged by a young woman with whom she was working—an avid reader of romance fiction and a helpful critic.

For Yvonne Whittal, there is no greater satisfaction than writing. "The characters become part of my life," she says, "and when I come to the end of each novel, realizing that I now have to part with my manuscript, it is like saying farewell to dear and trusted friends."

What readers say about Harlequin romance fiction...

"Harlequin books are the doorway to pleasure."

E.W., Hawthorne, California

"They are quality books—down-to-earth reading! Don't ever quit!"

G.F., Buffalo, Minnesota

"A pleasant escape from the pressures of this world."

C.T., Hickory, North Carolina

"Keep them coming! They are still the best books."

R.W., Jersey City, New Jersey

Harlequin Presents...

Romance novels that speak
the language of love known to
women the world over.

Harlequin Presents...

A distinctive series of dramatic
love stories created
especially for you
by world-acclaimed
authors.

NEVER BEFORE PUBLISHED

SUPERROMANCE®

NOW!

Your chance to receive all the books in this exciting new series the moment they come off the press!

BEST-SELLING SERIES

SUPERROMANCES are the newest best-sellers in the North American romance market.

And no wonder.

EXCITING!

Each SUPERROMANCE contains so much adventure, romance and conflict that it will hold you spellbound until the tumultuous conclusion.

DRAMATIC!

SUPERROMANCE gives you more! More of everything Harlequin is famous for. Spellbinding narratives...captivating heros and heroines...settings that stir the imagination.

1981 brings you...

2 SUPERROMANCES novels every other month.

Each volume contains more than 380 pages of exciting romance reading.

Don't miss this opportunity!

Complete and mail the Subscription Reservation Coupon on the following page TODAY!